ROGER PRICE'S
THE
TOMORROW PEOPLE

CHILDREN OF THE EVOLUTION

Iain McLaughlin

The Tomorrow People:
Children of the Evolution
Written by Iain McLaughlin
Published in 2024 by
Oak Tree Books
oaktreebooks.uk

in association with
Chinbeard Books

Editor: Paul Simpson
Commissioning/Sub-Editor: Barnaby Eaton-Jones

Cover artwork: Robert Hammond
Layout and Typesetting: Joe Larkins

Iain McLaughlin

The Tomorrow People

in

CHILDREN OF THE EVOLUTION

A Chinbeard Books / Oak Tree Books Original

Contents

For Helen, Iona, Chloe, Nathaniel, Jess and Zizzy…
my own Tomorrow People.

From the Author

The Tomorrow People is one of the TV shows I remember most from my childhood. I was six years old when it first appeared, and I was obsessed. I even made my own jaunting belt using my favourite snake belt, a cassette box covered in black tape, and a draughts counter from the old toy box (these were the original belts not the snazzy black and white design ones). I spent months desperately hoping to break out, but I never did.

I watched every series religiously, hurrying home from school to catch each episode and always checking with *Look-In* to see when a new series (repeats were equally acceptable) might be starting – or to catch the fantastic comic strip adventures of the Tomorrow People in that mag's pages.

More than forty years later, those fabulous adventures I watched on the old family telly are still imprinted on my mind. Yes, they were limited by their budget (not that the young me noticed) but they weren't limited in imagination or ambition. They went to space, to Tibet, to Germany, to the Highlands…

What I've tried to do is write a story that feels like it belongs with those classic old episodes. If you want to imagine it as the novelisation of an unmade TV story, great. You can think of it either done on a 1976 TV budget or if Thames had won the Pools and put a few bob into the story – it's up to you… it's your imagination.

Let your imagination take you back to Tomorrow…

The Tomorrow People

If you've never met the Tomorrow People before…
their names are John Dixon, Stephen Jameson,
Elizabeth M'Bondo, and Mike Bell. If you met them,
they would seem like ordinary young people, but
they are anything but ordinary. They call themselves
The Tomorrow People because they are a new stage
in human evolution named homo superior. The
Tomorrow People have developed incredible new
abilities. The process of gaining these powers is
called "breaking out" and happens when Tomorrow
People are in their early teens.

Tomorrow People can talk to each other through
telepathy using the power of their minds. They can
also move objects using their minds, using the power
of telekinesis. Their minds also give them the ability
to teleport themselves from one place to another by
the power of thought, a process they call 'jaunting'.

To assist with the complexities of jaunting, they use specially designed jaunting belts which help them with long distance or complex jaunts. However, if they can see their destination or picture, in their thoughts, the belts are not needed.

While the Tomorrow People have developed these incredible abilities, their evolution has left them opposed to killing. They always seek a thoughtful, peaceful resolution, even to the most aggressive situations. But they never back down from doing what is right and use stun guns, which render their targets unconscious, to defend themselves.

There have been other Tomorrow People who have left Earth to work with the Galactic Federation on its immense space station known as the Trig. The Galactic Federation have taken a keen interest in Earth and the Tomorrow People, gifting them a living biotronic computer known as TIM. The computer has been installed in the Tomorrow People's base, the Lab, which was built by John beneath an abandoned London Underground station. Originally just a meeting place, the Lab has grown and now has sleeping quarters and other facilities, allowing for longer stays.

Though they try to exist in secret, away from the eyes of humanity, the Tomorrow People do have friends who have not broken out but still try to help. The Tomorrow People guard their existence carefully, knowing that not everyone will welcome this new evolution of humanity.

With thanks to Roger Price and Brian Finch.

THE TOMORROW PEOPLE

CHILDREN OF THE EVOLUTION

1: Unnatural Selection

A slightly disinterested-looking man in a dull brown suit and a ghastly tie was standing in front of an impressive building, giving a news report. He had the look of a man who had landed the booby-prize when work assignments were being handed out for the news broadcast that day.

Despite being less than enamoured of his task, the reporter was trying to give it his all to make the story interesting. His name was John Donald and, while he dreamed of being the next Reggie Bosanquet or Alastair Burnet and hosting *News at Ten*, he knew deep down that he was only ever going to be the reporter who was relegated to the lightweight fluff pieces, and whose name nobody could ever remember. He wasn't convinced that even his wife and kids remembered his name most days.

'Thank you, Reggie. Yes, there is a new exhibition

opening tonight here at the Natural History Museum. Given the museum's links to Charles Darwin it is hardly a surprise that the exhibition focuses on evolution, on man's past, and perhaps even on our future.'

The picture froze. It wasn't on a TV screen but seemed to hang in space over a rather futuristic table on which colours oozed and ebbed, changing shape and hue like a living thing. Similarly fluid hemispheres and pipes hung from the ceiling. It was all part of a futuristic room far beyond the reach of the local 1970s technology, and yet four young people stood in this room, watching the screen.

They were a unique group, each of them possessing the telepathic and telekinetic abilities which marked the next stage in mankind's development. They called themselves the Tomorrow People and the room they stood in was the main room of the Lab, their base deep under London.

Elizabeth, an intelligent, attractive dark-skinned woman in her early twenties, watched the screen intently. 'The future of humanity? Are they talking about us?'

Stephen, a good-looking lad in his late teens, clad in jeans and a sweater, grinned at Elizabeth's words. 'An exhibition all about us?'

The youngest of the group laughed. 'That's good for the ego.' His name was Mike, and he spoke with a noticeable London accent. He had a mop of dark hair, a cheeky grin and wore a blue denim jacket over a bottle green T-shirt with a sort of target logo on the front.

'Your head's quite big enough, thank you,' said John, the oldest and most serious of the four. He was dressed in sensible trousers and a jumper.

Stephen feigned outrage in Mike's defence. 'You can't talk to him like that,' he protested. 'Mike's a rock superstar.'

Mike scowled at his friend, completely aware that he was being wound up. 'Shut up.'

'You'll be top of the charts one of these days,' Elizabeth said encouragingly. She knew how much playing with his band, the Fresh Hearts, meant to Mike, and she was still young enough to recognise that the band were actually rather good.

'Maybe,' Stephen added, not quite ready to let the teasing stop.

John shook his head resolutely. 'I'm saying nothing.'

A slightly mechanical, but not quite artificial voice floated from all around the room. 'And I have no opinion on popular music,' it said. This was

TIM, the biotronic computer which ran the Lab and helped the Tomorrow People in countless ways every day. Though undoubtedly a computer, TIM was far more like a living being; capable of original thought and of expressing its fondness and concern for the Tomorrow People.

'Good dodge, TIM,' Stephen said appreciatively.

'I thought so,' TIM agreed.

As usual, it was John who brought a serious tone back to the conversation. 'We're getting a bit off topic,' he said, sounding stuffier than he intended. 'I think it might be worth visiting the opening of this exhibition tonight.'

Elizabeth nodded. She had been thinking the same thing. 'I agree.'

The idea also appealed to TIM. 'I would be intrigued to know how the man behind the exhibition managed to land such a prestigious event.'

TIM's interest caught John's attention. 'What do you mean?' he frowned.

Onto the screen, TIM conjured up images of less-than-reliable looking magazines, such as *Out There*, as he continued: 'Until recently, Professor Marchwood was known for his more outlandish views and opinions on evolution.'

'What kind of outlandish?' John asked before wincing, as the magazine on screen changed to *Bigfoot Bulletin*. The magazine's cover was garish with a horrific painted version of the Bigfoot dripping blood from its mouth.

'Well,' TIM explained, 'he is most famous for his expeditions searching for the Yeti and for Bigfoot.'

'Oh…' Elizabeth said, sounding thoroughly disappointed, 'that's not promising.'

But TIM was not finished. 'That was until two years ago when he began publishing papers of a far more serious nature.'

The screen changed again, this time showing respectable newspapers and magazines such as *The Times*, the *Chronicle*, the *Courier* and *Science Today*, all of them carrying articles by Professor Josiah Marchwood.

'Well, this should be an interesting night out for us,' Stephen said. Nobody was quite sure if he was serious or not.

Mike frowned. 'Tonight?' he asked uncomfortably.

'Yes,' John nodded. 'Is that a problem?'

Mike sniffed and shrugged uncomfortably. 'Well, it's just that we have a gig, remember?'

John looked back at his young friend blankly. 'A *gig*?'

Mike tried again. Pulling John into the 1970s really could be a drag. 'You know, a concert.'

'Oh.' John nodded his understanding. 'Your band.'

'Yeah,' Mike nodded. 'Like Stephen said, we're playing tonight.' He grinned cheekily. 'Sorry. I'll have to skip the office outing.'

John cleared his throat. 'Well, I don't want to be called a fuddy-duddy...'

'Nobody'd ever call you that,' Mike said, failing dismally to sound sincere.

'Not unless it was suddenly 1950,' Stephen added.

John straightened his back and looked around the smirking faces of his friends with a great show of long-suffering dignity. 'If it will stop you lot calling me a stick in the mud, you can go and play with your band,' he told Mike. 'Just don't make a habit of missing your responsibilities with us.'

'I won't,' Mike promised with a grin, 'but I'm pretty sure the three of you can handle a night in a museum without me.'

'I should think so, too,' John agreed.

Mike hurried off towards the jaunting pad. 'Try not to miss me too much.'

John looked after his young friend with a bland expression on his face. 'If you're playing that stuff you pass off as music, I won't miss you at all,' he quipped lightly.

Elizabeth stifled a laugh. 'Don't listen to him, Mike. You're very good and you know it.'

'Thanks, Elizabeth,' Mike answered. 'At least *you're* young enough to recognise talent when you hear it.'

With that, he clasped his hands to the stylish black and white belt he – and all of the other Tomorrow People – wore. His mind was focused on his bedroom at home, and he faded from the jaunting pad before arriving, an instant later, back in his bedroom. With a smile he noticed that his mum had laid out the jeans and T-shirt he wanted to wear for the gig. Glancing at his watch, he was pleased to see that he had time for something to eat before the band was due to meet.

The Natural History Museum – sometimes dubbed "a cathedral of nature" – was considered, by the majority of those in-the-know, to be the most important centre of natural history research, as well as storage of specimens and artefacts relating to earth sciences (such as botany, zoology and archaeology). The public display area, which often hosted skeletons of exotic animals or fossilised displays of dinosaurs, had long since become a favourite destination for tourists and the curious. Millions of specimens were safely stored in the museum's vaults, as reminders of species that had sadly slipped into extinction, or as vital objects used in research into Earth's living past.

It looked as if a large percentage of the museum's open spaces had been dedicated to Professor Marchwood's exhibition. Various sections showed artefacts dating back to the earliest evolution of man in Africa, with several different evolutionary offshoots given their own sections of the presentation. The displays were diverse, with cave painting, skeletons, realistic wax dummies in tableaus of family groups, or scenes of early men hunting. A section to the side was marked THE FUTURE OF MAN in futuristic type. The front of the exhibition had been devoted to chairs arranged in rows for the visitors to sit in, with a small podium facing them. A large and inviting buffet ran down one side by the seating. A good number of the seats were already filled, primarily by an older, academic crowd, though other ages were sprinkled around, mostly in a group discussing the display.

'Busy, isn't it?' Elizabeth said, looking around the museum from the doorway.

John, Elizabeth and Stephen wandered further into the hall.

'That's heartening,' John said. 'It's good to see people taking an interest in science.'

'And those of us who were just dragged along,' Stephen added cheerfully with an impudent grin.

John didn't return the smile. 'If you don't want to be here…'

Stephen held his hands up to placate his older friend. 'I'm just joking.'

Elizabeth has noticed that the venue was getting busier and nodded towards some empty chairs. 'I see some seats over there.'

Stephen followed her gaze and started off in that direction. 'I'll go and blag them.'

'Blag?' John echoed with dismay at Stephen's use of slang.

Elizabeth chuckled to herself. 'You know, I'm never quite sure if you really *are* a stuffy old…'

'…fuddy-duddy…' John supplied helpfully.

'…fuddy-duddy,' Elizabeth accepted with a smile, 'or if you just put it on for Mike and Stephen.'

A little smile tugged at the corner of John's mouth. 'Excellent.'

'In what way?' Elizabeth asked.

John looked around the room, carefully taking in every detail. 'Well, you know me better than they do and if you don't know if I'm being serious or not, neither will they.'

Elizabeth gave a brief laugh. 'You're an old sly-boots.'

'Guilty as charged,' John answered happily. His eyes stopped wandering as they found Stephen, who had plonked himself in a chair and was pointing to the empty row beside him. 'Stephen's got those seats. Shall we?' He ushered Elizabeth to lead the way and followed her to their seats.

Professor Marchwood was a small man of average height with a receding hairline. Such hair as he still possessed was rather frizzy and greying from a bright ginger. He wore a neat grey suit and a pair of black shoes which had been polished until they gleamed. He should have been in every way unremarkable. A figure that could fit in with thousands of other suited figures who bustled from the Tube to their offices, following the same routine every day. But

Marchwood was more compelling than that. He had an air of energy about him that made him really stand out.

In front of a full gallery at the National History Museum, Marchwood looked like a man in his element, twinkling eyes running round the room, making just enough contact with everyone present for them to feel like he was talking just to them.

He threw his arms wide to greet his audience.

'Ladies and gentlemen, welcome to the opening of this exhibition, of which I am really extraordinarily proud.' He paused as a polite ripple of applause filled the room. 'Little more than a hundred years ago, Charles Darwin challenged the world with his extraordinary "The Origin of Species", in which he postulated his theory of evolution. Now, barely more than a century later, we accept evolution as a fact, as readily as we expect and accept the rising and setting of the sun.' He paused, apparently waiting to see if anyone would be foolish enough to argue against evolution. He appeared slightly disappointed when no-one did, so he continued. 'But evolution is not an easy or simple matter. The phrase "survival of the fittest" is often used to describe the evolutionary process. But sometimes it is not the fittest but the wisest and the most cunning that survive. Sometimes it is those who most nimbly adapt and change… those who evolve most adeptly to suit their conditions.'

Marchwood had lifted his voice in a slight crescendo, encouraging his audience to clap again. That was the natural break he had prepared, so that he could move on to the next part of his speech.

'In the past, humans – men such as we are – out-evolved other early forms of man, such as Neanderthal man and the Denisovans, by simply being more intelligent.' He waved his hand, indicating the display around them. 'In this exhibition, you will see examples from many species of evolutionary winners and losers. Those who survived and thrived and those who were unfortunately dead ends.'

He paused, encouraging another smattering of applause before continuing. He obviously had a taste for the theatrical.

'And what of the future?' he asked. 'It is surely only the most arrogant of minds that can imagine that humanity has already reached the zenith of our evolutionary journey. What is next for mankind?' He left the question hanging in the air as he cast his eyes round the room, carefully looking at every face present. 'We have lost most of the hair from our bodies – well, except for Sean Connery and Burt

Reynolds…' He took a breath as the expected, polite laugh came. 'Will we lose all of our hair because we no longer really need it? Oh dear, that's causing panic among the world's hairdressers, isn't it?' He smiled as another laugh came, more naturally this time. The audience was relaxing. As he carried on, his voice became persuasive and questioning. 'But the question remains, how will *we* change? Bald? Shorter? Taller? Will we really grow square eyes from watching too much TV, as our mothers warn us?' Another laugh came but the audience was now more interested in his words than in laughter. 'And will the changes all be physical, or will they also be mental? How will our *minds* evolve?' He left that question in the air for a long, long moment, giving it weight and gravitas, before the impish smile tugged again at the corners of his mouth. 'I do hope you are just as excited by this exhibition and the questions it raises as I am, as we all are here. Enjoy the exhibition – and enjoy the buffet. It's rather good.'

Professor Marchwood's speech had ended to a healthy response from the gathered audience. While

13

still joining in the clapping, the Tomorrow People were already telepathically communicating among themselves.

'Well,' Elizabeth thought to her friends, 'that was…'

'Wasn't it just?' John agreed. 'I think TIM should do some real digging on this Professor Marchwood.'

'Just what I was thinking,' Elizabeth concurred.

'And I was thinking that buffet looks good,' Stephen added cheekily to his friends.

'Really, Stephen…' John began disapprovingly, but Stephen mentally interrupted.

'And Professor Marchwood's assistant is standing beside it,' Stephen continued. 'Might be an idea to grab a chat with him while I grab a sandwich.'

The clapping had stopped, and the crowd was splitting into small groups, a low murmur of conversation building. To fit in, Elizabeth switched the conversation to speaking out loud. 'Good thinking,' she told Stephen.

The young man grinned. 'I'm not just here for my looks, you know.'

'That's a relief,' John muttered.

Stephen frowned, but there was no malice in the exchange, just the good-natured teasing that only comes from close friends. 'Cheek.'

John raised his eyebrows innocently. 'And you said Mike had a big head.'

Stephen ignored the comment and headed off towards the buffet. 'Back in a bit.'

As Stephen moved away, John focused his thoughts on contacting the Lab. 'TIM, did you hear what was said about Professor Marchwood?'

The computer's voice replied in their minds almost immediately. 'I am already scanning the media database for all mentions of him.'

'Good,' John answered. 'Let us know what you find out.'

'I will,' TIM confirmed.

John scanned the room until he spotted Professor Marchwood standing near his little podium, in conversation with an elderly, academic-looking couple. Other little groups had gathered nearby, waiting in turn to speak with Marchwood. 'I think we should have a word with the professor,' John said.

'I agree,' Elizabeth nodded, but she caught his arm before he could move, 'though perhaps we should take a minute and mingle our way there and not be too obvious.'

Stephen had found the buffet and was thoroughly impressed by the range of food on offer. He had quickly set about piling a plate high with sandwiches, sausage rolls and even chicken drumsticks. He was pleased that it was a proper plate rather than a flimsy paper one, too. The museum was putting effort into the event.

Looking along the table, Stephen saw what looked like roast beef poking from between two slices of neatly cut bread. One more wouldn't do any harm, would it? And it meant he had to open a conversation with the suited man who had been pointed out as Professor Marchwood's assistant.

'Excuse me,' he said politely to the man in the suit. 'Would you mind if I grab one of those?' He pointed at the platter of roast beef sandwiches.

'Not at all.' The assistant's stern face broke into a friendly grin. 'They're excellent. I had one earlier.' He moved aside to give Stephen the space he needed to pluck one of the sandwiches away and drop it on his own plate.

'Thanks,' Stephen said. 'I haven't eaten today. Bit of a rush to get here.'

That seemed to please the assistant. 'We will take that as a compliment,' he said. 'I'm gratified to see young people here.' He looked around at the rest of the crowd, nearly all of whom were obviously more mature. 'These events tend to attract an older crowd.'

Stephen had followed the man's gaze. They had all spotted the age of the crowd when they had come in. 'I suppose we are the youngest here.'

The assistant nodded. 'I saw you arrive earlier. Three of you.' His eyes fell on John and Elizabeth, who had moved closer to the professor. 'Is that an older brother?'

In many ways John *was* like an older brother to Stephen. He was a friend, a confidant, someone Stephen could turn to for advice, and someone he could rely on, no matter what. But then at other times he felt much older than a brother would have been. 'More like a father sometimes,' Stephen quipped. 'But no, we're just good friends really, all three of us.'

'Excellent.' That seemed to satisfy the suited man. 'And, may I ask, what is your interest in evolution?'

'We're interested in all forms of science really,' Stephen replied evasively, 'and Elizabeth is always looking for something new to interest her class.'

'Ah, she is a teacher?'

Stephen took a bite out of his sandwich, aware that the assistant was asking questions instead of answering them. He chewed for a few moments to gather his thoughts.

'Yes,' he replied between chews. 'This sandwich really is good.'

'I told you they were.' The assistant beamed.

Stephen took the opportunity given by the lull caused by his eating to change the direction of the conversation. 'So, what's your part in the exhibition?'

'I'm Professor Marchwood's assistant,' the man answered. 'My name is Baines.'

Stephen accepted the outstretched hand and shook it. 'I'm Stephen, Stephen Jameson.'

'A pleasure,' Baines replied.

Stephen looked at the nearest exhibit, a tableau of cavemen. 'This is all a bit of a change for the professor, isn't it?' he asked. 'He used to be a bit more… you know… *out there* with his ideas.'

'Is it the "out there" material that interests you?' Baines asked with an understanding smile.

'Well,' Stephen answered sheepishly, 'who isn't interested in Bigfoot?' He had given just enough enthusiasm to that question that he knew he sounded like a schoolboy interested in monsters. 'Though I'm interested in the more mainstream part of the professor's research too,' he added, making sure Baines would think he was trying to sound serious.

Baines took on a rather staid tone and Stephen realised the man was reciting something he had prepared earlier. 'A scientist has to ask questions, Stephen, and then when he gets his answers… that's when he's able to have a moment like this.'

'I suppose you're right,' Stephen answered. 'He must be really proud of this evening.'

'I hope so,' Baines said, casting his gaze towards the professor, who was now engaged with two familiar young people. 'Ah, he's telling your friends about it.'

Professor Marchwood was indeed talking to John and Elizabeth, who had patiently waited for a chance to slide into his orbit. He was proving to be jolly and friendly company, quite open to discussing his rather colourful research past. 'Yes, yes, I did rather look into, shall we call it, the more *esoteric* side of things in the past.'

'What was the draw there?' Elizabeth asked.

Marchwood grimaced self-consciously. 'Well, I could be glib and say I was young, and we do enjoy more fanciful ideas when we're young.' The grimace turned into an appealing, friendly smile. 'I mean, who hasn't seen a horror film about the Abominable Snowman or read about Bigfoot?'

John was not distracted by the professor's affable manner. 'But that's not the real answer?'

'No, not at all,' Marchwood chuckled self-consciously.

'Are we allowed to ask what the real answer is?' Elizabeth asked.

'Be careful,' John warned archly. 'Elizabeth might ask you to show your working in the margin.'

The Professor frowned. 'Pardon?'

Elizabeth laughed out oud. 'John's making fun of me being a teacher.'

'A teacher? How marvellous,' Professor Marchwood enthused. 'I can't think of a more noble way to spend your life. You should bring your class to the exhibition.'

Elizabeth bobbed her head, graciously accepting the offer. 'I'll talk to our Headteacher about it. Thank you.'

'My pleasure,' Marchwood beamed.

John gently nudged the conversation back to Marchwood's earlier work. 'You still haven't told us what made you abandon the slightly more unusual theories you used to investigate.'

'Oh, I haven't abandoned anything,' Marchwood said genially.

'You haven't?' Elizabeth frowned.

'No.' Marchwood shook his head and then enthusiastically set about explaining. 'You see, I was asking the serious questions back then, too. It's just that the more abstract ones caught all the attention. Nobody was interested in the hard work being done by me at the same time.'

'I think scientists through the ages would recognise that,' John offered reassuringly.

Marchwood seemed to appreciate the comment and continued. 'The thing is that you have to ask lots of questions as a scientist or a historian.' He took a deep breath before carrying on, positively sparkling with enthusiasm. 'If Darwin hadn't asked odd questions, his theory would never have been researched and accepted as it is now. No-one would know how man evolved. If you went back to Darwin's time and simply asked about Neanderthal Man, well, they'd have locked you up.'

The man's enthusiasm was infectious. 'You know, Professor,' John said, 'I love to see someone so immersed in their work.'

Marchwood accepted the compliment happily. 'Thank you.'

Elizabeth had recognised something in John's voice that Marchwood hadn't. There was just a slight suggestion that it was time to end the chat. 'We could talk to you all night,' she told Marchwood, 'but I think we'd wind up as extinct as Neanderthal Man if we did. There are a lot of people eager to talk to you.'

John agreed. 'Elizabeth's right. We shouldn't monopolise your time.'

Marchwood shook their hands. 'Thank you for your interest. I do appreciate seeing young people at events like this.' He glanced across at the buffet table, where Stephen was putting a few extra sandwiches on his plate. 'Now, I suggest you rescue your young friend from my assistant, Baines.' He leaned close and said conspiratorially, 'He's terribly efficient but the man is a terrible bore.'

'I think we probably need to rescue your buffet from Stephen,' John said, as Stephen's eyes fell on the sausage rolls again.

'He's a growing boy,' Elizabeth reminded John playfully, 'though he'll be growing round the waist if he eats all of that.'

Stephen had noticed his friends looking at him and led Baines across to join Professor Marchwood's little group.

'Hello, Stephen,' John said dryly. 'Finished eating?'

'Well, you hurried me out before I could actually eat,' Stephen protested, but he did offer the plate to John and Elizabeth.

Baines gave Stephen a friendly smile. 'It was very nice meeting you.'

'Shall we have a look around?' John asked his friends.

'Good idea,' Elizabeth agreed, plucking a roast beef sandwich from Stephen's plate. He looked peeved to see it go.

'Enjoy the exhibition,' Marchwood said, as the Tomorrow People said their goodbyes and moved away. He waited until the trio were out of earshot before speaking to his assistant. 'What do you think, Baines?'

Baines didn't answer the question but instead asked one of his own. 'What were those two talking about?'

Marchwood's lips pursed as he recalled the conversation. 'They asked a lot of questions… particularly about my interest in things like the Yeti.'

'Young people are often interested in that sort of thing,' Baines answered dismissively.

'Yes,' Marchwood replied, 'but they were sceptical.'

'That's rather unusual,' Baines replied, but his face gave away nothing.

'Isn't it?' Marchwood said. 'What about the other one?'

Baines rubbed at the end of his nose. 'He had questions, too.'

Marchwood watched the Tomorrow People pass by an elderly couple and make small talk. 'What do you think?'

'Could be innocent enough,' Baines answered. 'Nonetheless, I think we should keep an eye on them.'

Marchwood chuckled to himself. 'That's the third set of guests you've said we should watch.'

'I don't care if it's the thirty-third.' Baines's voice was suddenly sharp and cold. 'We'll watch them *all*, if we have to.'

John, Elizabeth and Stephen had wandered away towards one of the more quieter, out-of-the-way parts of the exhibition. They made a show of looking at a display of early human tools and weapons while talking telepathically.

'So, what was the professor like?' Stephen mentally asked his friends.

Elizabeth answered, while maintaining the charade of looking at the display. 'Charming, funny.'

'Not as well informed as he thinks,' John added. The others recognised that there was something behind John's words.

Elizabeth's eyebrow rose curiously. 'In what way?'

John's reply was also being heard in the Lab, where TIM had joined the conversation. 'Some of the details here are a bit off,' John thought to his friends. 'What do you make of it, TIM?'

The computer's response was immediate. 'I would need to link with you to fully see what you see.'

'We'll do that back at the Lab,' John replied. 'Right, let's all keep our eyes open, see as much as you can, remember everything.'

'All right,' Stephen agreed.

Elizabeth was curious about Baines. 'By the way, what was the assistant like?'

'Friendly,' Stephen answered.

'Is that all?'

Stephen thought for a moment. 'Not really. He asked a lot of questions.'

'About what?' John asked quickly. Everyone could sense that he was suspicious.

'About us,' Stephen answered. 'About the people here.'

'So did the professor,' John mused.

Elizabeth looked for a simple, reasonable explanation. 'They could just be showing a natural curiosity about the people coming to the exhibition.'

'That's possible,' John conceded. 'Scientists who run these kinds of exhibitions are always looking for someone willing to fund their next project.'

Everyone could hear the humour in Stephen's thought. 'They needn't look at me. I'm broke.'

John cast him that look, which Stephen could never decipher as to whether the older Tomorrow Person was serious or not. 'Don't think about using your powers to rob a bank.'

'Wouldn't think about it,' Stephen answered glibly. 'Though obviously you have, or you wouldn't have mentioned it.'

'Funny man,' John responded sourly.

Elizabeth brought the bickering to a stop. 'Shall we continue looking around?'

But Stephen was already reaching out telepathically to the absent Tomorrow Person. 'How's it going, Mike?'

Mike replied with just one word and the crashing sound of cymbals. 'Drumming.'

Clearly the gig was still in progress and Mike was busy.

'Best leave him,' Stephen said.

John's eyes had wandered to the sign with futuristic lettering. 'Let's take a look at what the professor thinks the future of humanity might be.'

Baines's wristwatch buzzed. Looking down at it, he saw the dial lit up in a glowing red.

'Definitely some sign of activity,' he said.

Marchwood nodded. 'So, it worked.'

'You thought it wouldn't?' Baines asked, sounding irritated that Marchwood might have had doubts.

'No,' Marchwood replied easily. 'Just curious who it is, that's all.'

Baines cast his eyes around the room. 'Well, we will find out in time.'

Halfway across London, Mike and his band, the Fresh Hearts, were having a really good night. The youth club was full, and the crowd was bouncing with energy. The band had been building a reputation for months and this was their biggest show so far... and it was going well. As the drummer, it was Mike's job, along with the bass guitarist, to drive the rhythm of the band through their songs. He had exchanged a couple of quick glances with his bass player and had seen his friend smiling.

He was right. The band were having a good night.

Just for a moment Mike thought about Stephen's message and wondered how the other Tomorrow People were doing in the museum, but he abandoned the thought after a moment. He was pretty sure they weren't having nearly as much fun as he was.

'Is this what we're going to look like?' Stephen asked.

In the museum, the three Tomorrow People had stopped in front of a glass display case with what looked like the wax replica of a small humanoid figure stood inside.

Stephen shook his head, unimpressed by humanity's future. 'Short, fat and bald? That looks like my grandad.'

'A very progressive man,' Elizabeth said.

Stephen shook his head firmly. 'You never met him. Hope you keep it that way.' *Progressive* was not a word he would ever have used to describe that grandfather.

Elizabeth looked at the little humanoid's extended skull. 'A bigger brain?'

'Oh, definitely,' Stephen agreed, trying to sound as if he knew what he was talking about. 'Not loving the spindly arms, though.'

'No,' John joined this conversation for the first time. 'I'm not loving this at all.' He sounded worried.

'Why?' Elizabeth asked.

John nodded his head towards the figure in the case. 'I've met one of these before.'

Stephen immediately frowned. 'What?'

'Let's not look surprised,' John warned him telepathically. 'Act normally.'

John nodded his head towards the small figure in the glass case. 'This is a Kultullan,' he thought to his friends. 'I saw one at the Galactic Federation last year.'

The name obviously triggered a memory for Elizabeth. 'Oh, yes, I've heard of them,' she answered. 'They were in negotiations to join the Federation.'

John's eyes didn't move from the immobile figure inside the glass. He stared at the small wrinkles in the flesh, the pores, the imperfections that nature would provide but which would never have been allowed by an artist. He had no doubt that this was the body of a real Kultullan. 'Did they join in the end?' he asked telepathically.

'I don't know,' Elizabeth answered. 'I can jaunt back to the Lab and check... talk to the Federation directly if necessary.'

'No,' John countered quickly. Leaving suddenly might arouse suspicion. 'Let's take it easy, see what else is here and then circulate back to the historical artefacts.'

In the Lab, TIM had accessed the databases of all the major national newspapers and press agencies. He was sifting through any back issues and articles that had been digitised anywhere, searching for anything relating to Professor Marchwood. Very few of the major outlets were digitised but over the years TIM had found his own ways to access information. He ordered every article or feature and began to build a comprehensive narrative of the professor's career.

In the museum, John, Elizabeth and Stephen had completed a full tour of the exhibition, which they had to admit was thoroughly impressive. It was full of quite fascinating displays and conveyed a good deal of information to the audience in an easily understandable manner.

The problem was that some of the information was very dubious.

John had begun moving the trio towards the exit.

'Have you seen enough?' Elizabeth asked telepathically.

'I think so,' John agreed. 'We should be on our way.' He caught Stephen's arm. 'On foot, Stephen. We don't want to alarm anyone.'

Stephen replied with the sourest look he could muster. 'I wasn't going to just disappear in front of the crowd.' Even telepathically, his voice dripped with the sarcasm that only a teenage boy can muster.

Abruptly, John switched to speaking out loud. 'Shall we go?'

He had seen Professor Marchwood approaching. The professor had noted their progress towards the door. 'Are you leaving so soon?' He sounded disappointed.

'Professor,' John smiled in greeting. 'Yes, it's getting late.'

'And this is a school night,' Elizabeth added apologetically. 'It'll take us all a little while to get home.'

'Ah, I understand,' the professor said sympathetically. He waved a finger around the hall before talking to Elizabeth. 'Please do talk to your Head about bringing your class to the exhibition.'

'I will,' Elizabeth promised.

John shook the professor's hand. 'Enjoy the rest of your evening.'

'By the way,' Stephen interrupted, 'which way to the Underground?'

Outside of the museum, John led Elizabeth and Stephen across Cromwell Road and onto Cromwell Place, heading towards South Kensington underground station.

John gave Stephen a withering look. '*Which way to the Underground* indeed?'

'Never hurts to throw up a bit of cover, does it?' Stephen answered innocently.

'No, I suppose not,' John conceded.

He sounded just a little suspicious that Stephen was making fun of him for being so strait-laced again, but he didn't sound too upset about that either. 'We should let TIM look at our memories of tonight,' he said.

They walked on, but instead of crossing the street towards the station, they turned right into the gloom of Cromwell Mews. Anyone following a few seconds behind them would have been startled to find the mews empty and quiet. The Tomorrow People had jaunted away.

Back in the Lab, John, Elizabeth and Stephen were seated at the table talking to TIM. Stephen was, to everyone else's shock, eating another sandwich, this time supplied by TIM.

'All right, TIM,' John said. 'We're ready to...' He stopped as a glass of juice appeared on the table in front of Stephen.

'Sorry,' Stephen grinned. 'I was just getting a drink.'

John's eyebrow rose. 'Did you get one for...' He fell silent as a mug of tea appeared in front of Elizabeth and another by his own hand. 'Oh, good man.'

'Thanks, Stephen,' Elizabeth said, taking a sip from her mug. 'Any other party tricks?'

'No, but if TIM could rustle up some chips...'

'After we've got this done,' John said firmly.

Stephen scrunched up his nose in mock disappointment but immediately laid his hands palm-down on the table. John and Elizabeth did the same.

'All right,' John said, 'everybody link minds.'

All three Tomorrow People opened their minds and began to share their memories of the evening inside the museum. They felt TIM's presence, sifting through their memories and causing the scents, sounds and tastes of the evening to return as fresh as if they were happening for the first time in that instant.

'You were right,' TIM said seriously. 'There are some fascinating inaccuracies in the material you saw at the museum.'

'Such as?' John asked.

'The suggestion that Neanderthal Man had the potential for advanced mental abilities.'

'Do we know he didn't?' Elizabeth asked.

'No, *we* know he did...' TIM answered, 'but humanity in general has no way of knowing this yet.'

'Science is based on deductions changing the known facts,' Elizabeth offered reasonably.

'But that doesn't explain the Kultullan,' John countered.

'Could it be a coincidence?' Stephen asked, though even he didn't sound convinced about it.

John shook his head. 'It would be a very large coincidence, and I don't believe in those.'

TIM cut in, bringing up a picture of an article from one of the previous Sunday papers onto the screen. It showed Marchwood in front of the museum. 'And I do not believe that Professor Marchwood is the author of these new theories and articles.'

John's brow furrowed into a frown. 'Why do you say that, TIM?'

'The linguistic stye is completely different,' TIM explained. The image on screen flicked between a number of newspaper and magazine articles. 'The syntax and structure of sentences is nothing like anything he wrote before. His choices in his vocabulary have also changed. They are undoubtedly the works of two different people.'

Elizabeth looked for an alternative explanation. 'And we're sure that is definitely Professor Marchwood we saw tonight?'

The image on screen changed again, this time showing a younger version of the man they had been speaking with. 'These press cuttings relate to his various expeditions and book launches in the past. It is undeniably the same man.'

'He could be passing off someone else's work as his own?' Elizabeth suggested.

John rubbed thoughtfully at his chin. 'Or it could be something more sinister than that.'

'What?' Elizabeth wanted to know.

John wrinkled his nose unhappily. 'I don't know,' he sucked on his lip for a moment, 'but I think we should pay that exhibition another visit tonight – after the museum closes.'

36

A little over an hour later, John, Elizabeth and Stephen were back in the Natural History Museum. They had jaunted into a quiet area by a side exit and used their telekinetic abilities to unlock the door. Once inside, they had found a quiet, shadowy place to hide as the museum began to close down for the night. Lights were switched off, leaving only a few small lights in each room to give security guards a guide as they patrolled the building. Slowly, the footsteps became fewer, and the museum fell into darkness and silence.

Stephen was first to become impatient about their inactivity. 'Why didn't we just jaunt in?'

'We don't know who's going to be wandering about,' John replied. 'We don't want to scare an innocent security guard, do we?'

Stephen saw the sense in the answer but couldn't resist quipping, 'Sounds like fun to me.'

John didn't see the funny side. 'Maybe we should go back to the Lab and bring Mike instead of you – when he eventually shows up.' John had seemed troubled that Mike's concert had gone on longer than expected.

'They were doing their last few numbers when I tried to contact him,' Stephen explained.

John gently put a hand on Stephen's shoulder to make sure he didn't move from their hiding place.

'Wait.'

'What?'

It was Elizabeth who answered. 'Security guard,' she thought to them.

Sure enough, the sound of a pair of heavy, booted feet echoed around the museum and a moment later the figure of a security guard appeared, slowly meandering on his patrol, looking bored. His body language spoke of a man who did not expect any trouble at his job that night.

The Tomorrow People waited until he had moved out of sight and his footsteps had faded from their hearing before they emerged from hiding and began making their way back through Professor Marchwood's exhibition.

John led his friends past some familiar displays. Though, in the near darkness, the shadows gave the tableaus of early cavemen a sinister edge. 'This way.'

'Pity we didn't bring torches,' Stephen said.

'It's light enough to see,' John countered firmly.

Elizabeth agreed. 'And they'd attract the guards.'

John's voice sounded in their heads. 'Talking of which…'

They paused as they heard another pair of booted feet echo in the corridors, but they were too far away to be a threat to their mission.

'I want to see that Kultullan,' John said, moving away along the display and turning towards the section relating to the future of man. 'Over here.'

He stopped at the glass case and began running his fingertips over the corners, trying to find a weak spot in the seal.

'Let me.' Elizabeth flexed her hand and extended it, with a flat palm aimed at the seal between two of the sides.

'Can you open the case?' John asked.

A confused frown appeared on Elizabeth's face. 'No… John, I can't…'

John held his palm out to the glass. 'Let me try…' He looked startled and took a step backwards. 'No.'

Stephen looked from John to Elizabeth. 'What is it?'

'I can't use my powers to open the case,' Elizabeth said.

'Neither can I,' John confirmed. 'Try talking telepathically.'

Stephen closed his eyes and tried to communicate with his friends. 'I can't.'

Elizabeth shook her head. 'Neither can I.'

'Nor me,' John said. 'I don't know what's causing it, but I don't like it.'

Elizabeth looked around the museum nervously. It had suddenly become a far more menacing place for them. 'I agree. We should jaunt out.'

Almost in unison they touched their hands to their belts and focused their thoughts on the Lab.

Nothing happened.

They were still in the museum.

'I can't jaunt,' Stephen said.

'None of us can,' Elizabeth confirmed.

Even the normally calm John looked worried. 'Something's inhibiting all of our powers. We have to get out of here.'

But Elizabeth's head was turned away, listening. Running footsteps were getting closer. 'Security guards.'

John was already pushing his friends forward. 'Run.'

All three sprinted through the exhibition, moving away from the heavy footsteps of the guards.

'This way,' Stephen said, pointing away from the footsteps, but Elizabeth caught his arm.

'No. Over there,' she said, pointing to a more circuitous route back to the way they had come in.

'Can either of you jaunt yet?' John asked urgently.

Elizabeth closed her eyes briefly. 'No,' she answered. 'Something's still dulling my powers.'

The guard's heavy footsteps were getting closer. There was a real risk of them being caught before they made their escape.

'We need to get out of here,' Elizabeth said.

'Run,' John said, pointing round the next corner. He focused his thoughts on the Lab, searching for a familiar presence in his mind. 'TIM… TIM…'

In the Lab, TIM had been growing concerned by the lack of contact from the Tomorrow People in the museum. Abruptly, he was aware of… *something*.

Concentrating on the incoming sensation, he recognised it as John's thoughts trying to contact him, but it felt as if John was trying to reach him from a great distance or through some kind of interference.

'John?' TIM tried to reach John, boosting his abilities to the most powerful he could manage. 'I can't understand you.'

There was no reply. Instead of John's mind, all he could reach was a form of white noise in his mind.

There was no doubt that John and the others were in some kind of trouble. TIM turned his mind towards the one Tomorrow Person not in the museum.

'Mike...'

Mike's reply was distracted, his mind full of the rhythm of the song and making the finale to the song memorable. 'Just finishing the set,' came the answer.

TIM came straight to the point. 'The others are in trouble...'

As the band hit the final chord of their last song, a firework crackled, and a plume of smoke belched up in front of the drums. The crowd roared their appreciation.

As the smoke cleared, the audience saw that the drum kit was now empty.

Mike had disappeared.

They cheered louder in appreciation of this seemingly magic trick.

42

The crowd was still cheering in the club, but Mike was already back in the Lab. 'What is it, TIM?' he asked, hurriedly stepping off the jaunting pad. 'What happened to them?'

'I don't know, Mike,' TIM answered. He sounded worried. 'They went back to the museum to investigate but I can't contact them. Something is blocking me.'

'What can I do?' Mike asked.

John's attempt to get to the side door they had used to enter the museum had been thwarted by the presence of considerably more security guards in the building than they had expected. Two of them, both huge and muscular figures, blocked the hoped-for route to freedom.

'More guards over there,' John whispered, pulling his friends back towards the shadows.

'Look at their uniforms,' Elizabeth said. She was usually calm and assured but even she sounded nervous. 'Those aren't typical security guard outfits.'

John had seen something even more concerning. 'And guards don't usually carry guns.'

He was right, Stephen realised. The guards were all armed. 'We have *definitely* got to get out of here.'

John agreed and urged his young friend to lead the way back along towards the other side of the museum. They had barely made a few steps before a guard's voice echoed loudly through the museum. 'There they are!'

Stephen was still in the lead and ran hard for a doorway. 'This way.' The door was locked, and the handle wouldn't budge. 'Maybe not,' he muttered.

John hadn't even slowed. He hurried past his friends and took the lead. 'Turn left,' he hissed, turning into a darkened narrow space between two tall display cases. 'Down here.'

Elizabeth and Stephen followed John into the darkness, but they were just too slow, and the first security guard to arrive saw them disappear into the recessed area. He pointed out their hiding place to two of his colleagues who arrived moments later. 'There's no escape for them. That's a dead end.'

But, when they looked into the closed cul-de-sac, there was no-one there. The fugitives had vanished.

All four Tomorrow People stepped from the jaunting pad. Each of them showed a sense of relief at being safely back at their base.

'Thanks for that, Mike,' John said with some considerable feeling.

'Just in time,' Elizabeth added appreciatively, as Stephen slapped a grateful hand on Mike's shoulder.

'Thanks, Mike,' he said.

Having missed the night's events, Mike was even more confused than the rest. 'What was happening there?' he asked. 'As soon as I arrived, I felt all my powers disappear.'

'The same happened to us,' Elizabeth answered, sinking into a chair.

John leaned on the table wearily. 'There was a field dampening all telekinetic activity.'

Stephen removed a small rectangular box from his jaunting belt and placed it on the table. It was these booster boxes that Mike had handed to each of his friends as soon as they had joined him in the darkened recess between displays. He had been lucky that he had found his friends so quickly after his late arrival in the museum, and luckier still that John had seen him pointing to that darkened hiding place.

'How did the boosters get past that dampening effect?' Stephen asked.

John answered automatically, 'They're mechanical rather than based on our abilities.'

'I think that was aimed at me, John,' TIM interrupted gently.

'Oh, I'm sorry, TIM,' John answered ruefully.

'There is no need,' TIM said genially. There was no offence in his tone. 'Are your powers returning?'

'I don't know,' John answered. He thought for a moment. 'I feel normal.'

'That would be a first,' Stephen joked.

John scowled at his young friend. 'Your sense of humour is back to normal – unfortunately.'

Elizabeth extended a hand, and a school textbook lifted from a low table and floated through the air until it slid into her grasp. 'My powers are coming back.'

John took off the booster from his belt and placed it on the table before jaunting from one side of the Lab to the other. It was a short jaunt, but it was enough to show that his special abilities had returned. 'Mine too.'

'We're all back to normal?' Stephen sighed with relief.

'So, what now?' Mike asked.

'I'm not sure,' John answered honestly.

But Elizabeth was more certain about what

they had to do. 'We need another look inside that museum.'

'You're right,' John agreed, 'but not tonight.' He sighed and stifled a yawn. 'It's been a long day and we're all tired. Let's get some rest and we'll start again in the morning.'

Elizabeth woke next morning with a fully formed plan in her mind. She ran the idea round her brain as she showered and dressed, before presenting it to the other Tomorrow People in the Lab.

She was disappointed that her friends were not as enthusiastic as she was.

John was the first to voice his opposition. 'Elizabeth, I'm not at all sure about this plan of yours.'

'Neither am I,' TIM agreed, concern obvious in his voice.

In truth, Elizabeth was not surprised by her friends' opposition. She had expected some resistance, and so she calmly and efficiently laid out her reasoning. 'The professor invited me to bring my class, remember?'

'And we lost our powers in there, remember,' John argued immediately.

'I'm not likely to forget that in a hurry,' she answered, 'but I'll be in there during the day, surrounded by a class of kids and hundreds of other tourists.' John couldn't argue with that. 'And I doubt that anyone at the museum would expect last night's unwelcome visitors to come back as part of a school party.' John frowned but didn't answer, so Elizabeth continued, 'and Professor Marchwood might get suspicious if I didn't bring my class…'

John had not been at all convinced, but Elizabeth's logical, persuasive argument had swayed him and he had given way.

A few hours later, Elizabeth was standing outside the museum, with a boisterous class of school children.

She sent a telepathic message back to her friends in the Lab. 'We're just going in now,' she thought.

John's reply came back quickly. 'As soon as you start to feel anything is wrong, you get out of there.' He sounded brusque but Elizabeth knew that was just his concern showing.

Slipping quickly into teacher mode, Elizabeth began herding her pupils towards the museum's front door, pulling up Dave Wilkins and Peter Munro for playing the fool, and putting the entire class on a warning to be on their best behaviour.

The party had only just made it into the museum when Professor Marchwood's voice was heard, and he hurried across to join them.

'Good morning,' he clucked happily. 'It's Elizabeth, isn't it?'

'The professor's here,' Elizabeth thought back to the Lab, as she smiled at the professor. 'I'll stay in touch.'

She switched to speaking out loud and greeted Marchwood warmly. 'Hello, Professor. Lovely to see you again. And yes, I'm Elizabeth – to you, if not to my pupils here. In front of them I'm Miss M'Bondo, please. But it's nice of you to remember. You must have met a lot of people last night.'

'You and your friends are young, so you stood out,' Marchwood answered. 'I didn't expect you to come back quite so quickly.'

Was he hinting at the late night visit the previous night or innocently talking about the class outing? Elizabeth remained friendly and answered innocently, 'Well, I talked to the Head in the staff room, first thing, and she thought it would be an excellent outing for the children today.'

John's voice came from the Lab. He was also suspicious of the professor's question. 'Do you think he suspects anything, Elizabeth?'

'I don't know,' Elizabeth answered mentally.

'Please remain in constant touch,' TIM's voice chimed in.

'And use the booster to get out if you have to,' John added.

Apparently unaware that Elizabeth had been conducting two conversations, Professor Marchwood was continuing to be an effusive host. 'Would you like me to give your pupils a talk at some point in the visit?'

Elizabeth focused her attention on Marchwood and gave a broad smile. 'That would be lovely, thank you,' she said warmly. She looked around and saw the class beginning to drift and wander, as children are apt to do when unattended. 'Maybe I should round them up a bit first. They can get boisterous.'

'Very well,' Marchwood replied happily. 'I'll meet you later.' And with that, he bustled off deeper into the museum.

'All right, everyone,' Elizabeth said sternly, 'gather together, no running off on your own.' She turned her gaze to one particular boy, who had a mischievous look in his eyes. 'That means you, Gareth.'

The boy pouted miserably 'Awww.'

Elizabeth ushered her charges forward. 'Straight ahead. I want you all to take notes of what you see,' she told them. 'I'll be asking questions later.'

'Elizabeth?' John's voice sounded in her ear, 'what is…'

In the Lab, everyone was suddenly aware that the connection with Elizabeth had been cut off.

'I can't communicate with Elizabeth,' John said.

Stephen concentrated but to no avail. 'Neither can I.'

John was already pulling on a jacket and heading for the jaunting pad. 'Stephen, you come with me,' he said. 'Mike, we might need you to come to the rescue again.'

Mike hid his disappointment at having to wait behind and nodded his understanding. 'I'll be ready.'

John looked to Stephen. 'Let's go.'

Less than a minute after leaving the Lab, John and Stephen hurried into the National History Museum. It only took a few seconds for them to find Elizabeth's class. The group of children were looking around in confusion. Neither of them could see any sign of Elizabeth.

John turned to the nearest clump of pupils. 'Your teacher, where is she?'

Stephen recognised that John's demanding tone might be off-putting for these kids. Being closer to their age ,he was able to sound much friendlier. 'Do you know where Miss M'Bondo is?'

The children all shook their heads. 'No,' one of the boys said. 'She's vanished.'

2: Mysteries of the Mountains

'And what do you mean by 'she vanished'?' Stephen asked the question quickly to ensure John didn't have time to do so. For all that Stephen liked John and respected him, he knew that his friend could come across as brusque – and that would not help them with a bunch of schoolkids.

The boy, Gareth, answered the question. 'One minute she was behind us over there.' He pointed just behind them and then shrugged. 'Next time we looked, she was gone.'

'But you didn't see her disappear in front of you?' John corrected himself hurriedly, as he realised how that sounded. 'I mean, you didn't see her go anywhere?'

'No.' Gareth shook his head, though he was eyeing John with suspicion. 'Why you asking, mister?'

'We're friends of hers, that's all,' John answered.

Gareth immediately saw the opening for mischief. 'You her boyfriend?'

'Never you mind,' John answered so sharply that Gareth suspected the young man might be another teacher. 'Just carry on doing whatever she told you to do,' John instructed her class.

John and Stephen moved away from the gathered group of pupils, looking into the museum. 'So, they didn't see her jaunt out?' Stephen said.

John shook his head. 'No, but if she'd got out, she would have contacted us.'

Stephen looked at his friend worriedly. 'You think she's been caught?'

John chewed his bottom lips for a moment. 'Possible,' he said, noncommittally. 'Let's take a look around.'

The museum wasn't as busy as the previous night. 'There aren't many people here yet,' Stephen said. 'We should be able to see her if she's…'

John cut him off abruptly as he saw a familiar figure approaching. 'Quiet.'

Professor Marchwood was hurrying towards them, a pleased-looking expression on his face. 'Oh, all three of you are here?' he said happily. 'I only saw your friend earlier. I was just looking for her.'

54

'So are we…' Stephen began, but John cut him off sharply.

'Are we to assume she talked her Head into funding the trip?' he asked Marchwood.

The question seemed to surprise the professor. 'It seems so,' he answered, looking around the museum. 'Do you know where she is?'

'No, not at all,' John replied. 'We were on our way to a meeting and thought we'd have another look in.'

While John and Marchwood were talking, Stephen has been looking in every direction hoping to catch any hint of Elizabeth's whereabouts. 'I don't see her anywhere,' he said telepathically, 'or sense her.'

Professor Marchwood turned to Stephen. 'Did you say something?' he asked amiably.

Stephen stood still, frozen like a deer in the headlights for a moment, before answering with a muttered, 'No. Nothing.'

John's face slipped into an expression Stephen recognised. His friend's smile was pulled into a smile that was just too relaxed to be genuine. 'If you see Elizabeth, please tell her we said hello,' he said to Professor Marchwood.

He followed that with a very quick telepathic message to Stephen. 'I think we need to go.'

'What about the schoolkids?' Stephen answered, looking worriedly at Elizabeth's class, which had started to wander aimlessly.

John replied swiftly. 'We can phone their Head and say Elizabeth was taken ill.'

'All right,' Stephen agreed.

John's mind reached out to TIM. 'TIM, could you contact Elizabeth's school, please?'

TIM replied immediately. 'Of course, John.'

Professor Marchwood was looking at Stephen with interest. 'I'm sorry. Are you sure you didn't say anything?'

'Is everything all right?'

All three looked over to see the professor's assistant emerge from behind a tall display cabinet.

'Mr Baines,' John said coolly. 'I'm afraid we were just leaving.'

'Must you?' Baines asked.

'Work beckons, I'm afraid.' John ushered his friend towards the door. 'Come on, Stephen.'

'We shall certainly say hello to your friend if we see her,' the professor promised.

John gave a nod of thanks and waved a farewell. 'Goodbye.'

Outside, on the pavement, John took a deep breath.

'She definitely wasn't in there,' Stephen said, 'but I did sense *something*.'

'I sensed a few somethings,' John answered uncomfortably, 'including a sort of after-echo of whatever affected our powers last night.'

'Yeah, I felt that, too,' Stephen nodded. 'And what was the professor up to with that "did you say something" stuff?'

'Not here,' John said, leading the way across the street. 'Come on. Let's get back to the Lab. Maybe TIM can find a way to search for Elizabeth.'

Elizabeth was wakened by a screaming pain in her head. It felt as if her skull was being slowly pulled apart. Thankfully, after a few moments, the pain began to fade, and she was able to open her eyes and to slowly focus on her surroundings.

The last thing she remembered was being in the museum with her class of pupils. The children had just moved ahead of her and there had been... there had been... well, something overwhelming in her mind that had knocked her out in a fraction of a second.

Her eyes had now become accustomed to the low light, and she could take in the details of the room around her.

Instead of the clean, polished surfaces of the museum, she found herself in a small room – undoubtedly a cell – cut out of rough, mottled, grey rock. The walls and ceiling were uneven and had sharp pieces jutting out.

The floor was, thankfully, smoother and covered with straw. Elizabeth herself had been placed on a very basic wooden cot onto which a thin straw-filled mattress had been thrown. She was partly covered by a coarse blanket, which felt like old sack cloth.

She tried to sit up but was overcome by a vicious wave of dizziness and sank back to the uncomfortable mattress, waiting for the nausea to pass.

She tried to focus her thoughts, to think past the queasy sensation running through her. She tried to reach out with her mind to John and to TIM. As the nausea faded, her senses became sharper, and she realised that her powers were again being muted by whatever had affected her before.

Gritting her teeth and wincing, Elizabeth forced herself to sit up and then to stand. She swayed unsteadily but finally found her balance. Leaning on the wall for support, she slowly made her way across the room to the basic wooden door.

A small window was placed roughly at head height. Any thought of attempting to use it to escape was dispelled by the thin, solid, iron bars that were running vertically in the frame.

Carefully positioning herself in the shadow to the side of the door, Elizabeth peered out through the window into a corridor which was cut from the same rough stone as her cell. Other doors also led off the corridor but were, oddly, of varying types. Some were basic and wooden, while others seemed to be metallic and fitted snugly into metal frames. These futuristic doors looked more like airlocks.

Elizabeth's curiosity was stopped in its tracks as she heard the unmistakable sound of booted feet on the stone floor of the corridor. She took a step back, further into the shadows.

A moment later, the door was thrown open and two large men in menacing, paramilitary-style, black uniforms entered.

Elizabeth managed a few steps away from the door, but the guards were too fast for her, and they caught her easily.

Each of the guards took a tight grip on one of Elizabeth's arms and between them they dragged her, struggling, out into the corridor.

John and Stephen turned off a busy street into a quiet alley.

Stephen ran to keep up with his friend. 'You got us out of there pretty sharpish.'

'Yes, I did,' John agreed.

'You're not scared of the professor, are you?'

'No,' John answered carefully, 'but I have a suspicion about him.' He looked Stephen squarely in the eye. 'And so do you.'

'Can't deny that.' Stephen replied.

John touched his hands to his jaunting belt. 'Come on, let's get back to the Lab.'

A moment later, John and Stephen rematerialized on the jaunting pad in the Lab.

Mike was out of his chair and by the pad before they had fully appeared. 'Where's Elizabeth?' he asked.

John and Stephen moved to the table, always the natural hub of the Lab's main room. 'The kids in her class said she disappeared,' John explained.

Stephen took over. 'And then Marchwood and Baines turned up and John decided we had to get out of there.'

Mike was outraged. 'What? You left Elizabeth?'

John gave Mike a sharp look which quietened the younger man. 'I got us out of there because, on two occasions, he asked Stephen if he'd said something.'

Mike didn't understand. 'So?'

'John's right,' Stephen confirmed. 'I *had* said something – but I said it telepathically.'

John's eyes focused on the table, but his mind was racing, running through all the possibilities he could summon. 'I don't know if he was taunting us, sending us a message or what, but it was no more of a coincidence than that Kultullan they've got on display.'

As usual, Mike favoured a direct plan of action. 'We should go back in there and find out what he knows.'

'With thumbscrews?' John asked before shaking his head. 'No, I think this needs a more subtle approach.' He sucked on his bottom lip. 'If TIM here can manufacture me some press credentials and a background at a reasonable newspaper, I'll ask Professor Marchwood for an interview.'

'When are we going back there?' Stephen asked.

'*We're* not,' John answered. 'I am.'

Stephen shook his head. 'Not on your own, you're not.'

'Don't worry,' John said. 'TIM and I will stay in contact.'

'And I have increased the power in John's jaunting belt,' TIM added.

Mike didn't like the sound of being left on the sidelines again. 'What about us?' he asked, indicating Stephen and himself.

It was TIM who answered. 'I assume that you will be following up something John and I found last night after you went to bed.'

'What's that?' Mike asked.

'The style of the professor's writings changed immediately after his expedition to the Himalayas in search of the Yeti.'

Stephen looked at John in disbelief. 'You're sending us to look for the Abominable Snowman?'

'No,' John answered quickly, 'I'm sending you to find out what happened to him on that expedition.' His finger tapped the table reflexively. 'We need to know what changed about him.'

'And you think we'll find it there?' Mike asked.

John nodded. 'I think there's a better chance of finding the truth about that part of this puzzle over there, than there is of finding it here.'

Stephen looked to Mike and shrugged. 'All right, TIM. Break out the thermal undies.'

Elizabeth was going to be tortured.

She had seen any number of interrogations – and had been subjected to a few – since breaking out as a Tomorrow Person. As soon as she saw the long bench, which was tilted to an angle (with the various, menacing pieces of futuristic equipment directed at it), she knew what was in store for her.

The guards lifted Elizabeth onto the bench and secured straps around her biceps, holding her in place. A third guard had joined them, and he swung a device into position over Elizabeth's head. It reminded her of the laser she had seen used to threaten James Bond in the film that she had seen on TV at Christmas. While this wasn't a laser, it was going to aim *something* at her, and she was sure it wasn't going to be something pleasant.

'What are you doing?' Elizabeth asked the new guard. He didn't answer. 'I asked you a question. What are you doing? Why have you brought me here?'

The guard interrupted her harshly. 'You are here to answer questions, not ask them.'

'I am here because you kidnapped me,' Elizabeth shot back angrily.

The guard ignored her. 'You will answer our questions,' he said coldly. 'If you do not answer we will inflict pain into your mind.' He adjusted the device above Elizabeth's head. 'What is your name?'

Elizabeth stared at the guard, scrutinising the humanoid figure and searching for any sign that he might be anything other than human. The black uniform covered him from neck to toe and Elizabeth had to admit that she couldn't see anything in particular that screamed that this thug wasn't human. There was something about him, though, something in the way he carried himself that made her sure he was not.

'What's your name?' the guard repeated, his voice growing even harsher.

Elizabeth looked at him with disdain. 'I'll tell you nothing.'

'Incorrect,' the guard answered.

The device above Elizabeth's head pulsed and a screaming pain seared through her brain. It felt as if her skull was burning and being ripped apart. She set her jaw firmly and said nothing.

'You will tell us your name,' the guard stated.

Elizabeth forced her brain to work, forced her

mouth to form the words. 'No thanks. You're not my type.'

She didn't see the guard operate the controls, but the device pulsed again and the pain in her brain intensified, multiplied several times, extending from her brain out through her nerves all through her body.

'You will tell me your name.'

Elizabeth fought the pain. 'No.'

The demand became a hideous mantra. Every time Elizabeth didn't answer, the pain level was increased. 'Tell me your name. Tell me your name. Tell me your name.'

'No!' Just forcing out that one word left Elizabeth exhausted, but the onslaught continued.

'Tell me your name. Tell me your name. Tell me your name. How many of you are there? Tell me your name.'

Wait. That was different. What did that mean? Why that different question?

'Tell me your name. Tell me your name. Tell me your name.'

Elizabeth's eyes flickered and closed and her head lolled. The body sank into a lifeless pose.

The guard looked at his unconscious victim and sneered. 'Weak.'

Mike and Stephen stumbled their way up a rocky trail on the lower stretches of the Himalayan mountain, Makalu. It was the fifth highest peak in the world, standing around 27,825 feet at its summit. It was an odd shape, looking not dissimilar to a four-sided pyramid… a very cold and icy four-sided pyramid with flurries of snow blown across its faces by vicious, biting winds.

Even though they were already cold, with wind and snow attacking down at this lower level, neither Stephen nor Mike really wanted to imagine how freezing it must be at higher altitude.

'This road is ridiculous,' Mike grumbled, as he almost lost his footing in the loose shale underfoot.

'It's not a road,' Stephen answered, 'it's a path.'

Mike was a city boy, who had spent his entire life in the familiar and welcome concrete surroundings of London. 'It's not even a path,' he complained. 'It's a construction yard. Look at all these broken stones.' He almost lost his footing again.

Stephen caught his friend's arm to steady him. 'If you're not careful, you'll be looking at broken ankles.'

They reached a tight turn on the trail and, as they rounded it, they could see a small, traditional village up ahead. The locals all went about their business, paying little attention to their young visitors.

Stephen communicated back to the Lab. 'TIM, are you sure this is the village Professor Marchwood visited?'

TIM's voice replied with reassuring speed. 'It is mentioned in a number of articles about this expedition.'

A middle-aged local man, leading a pair of docile yak along the trail towards them, offered a friendly smile and said something in his native language.

'TIM, can you translate?' Stephen asked telepathically.

'Yes,' TIM replied immediately.

Stephen smiled at the local. 'Hello.'

The man returned the smile. 'Hello,' he said, his voice translated by TIM, 'welcome to our village.'

'Thanks.' Mike got straight to the point. 'We're interested in finding out about a man who was here,' he said. 'A professor. A scientist, maybe?'

The local chuckled, unimpressed. 'Lots of people come here now,' he said. 'Professors, climbers…'

'We're talking about Professor Marchwood,' Stephen said.

'Marchwood?' The man certainly recognised the name.

'You remember him, then?' Mike asked.

'Yes.' An odd look appeared on the Tibetan man's face. '*Everybody* here remembers him.'

'Why?' Mike pressed.

'Strange ideas,' the man laughed. 'Strange thoughts.' He laughed even louder as he remembered the odd little scientist.

'Strange ideas?' Stephen continued to press, 'About what?'

The man wafted a hand up towards the peak of the mountain. 'About Meh-teh. About Dzu-teh.'

Stephen shook his head. 'What are those?'

The Tibetan thought for a moment, trying to call the words to mind. 'You call them Yeti,' he said. 'The Abominable Snowmen.'

That matched what they had already learned about the professor. 'He came here searching for them.'

'A lot of people come looking for them.' The Tibetan shrugged. 'It is good for the tourist business.'

Mike continued pushing for answers. 'What was strange about Professor Marchwood's ideas?'

The Tibetan, a friendly and cheerful man by nature, shook his head sadly. 'He thought he could talk with the Meh-teh. Maybe that he could catch them, bring them into our world.'

'And that won't happen?' Stephen asked.

The Tibetan looked at his young visitors with sympathy. 'Men have tried to capture the Meh-teh for hundreds of years,' he said, 'but they do not find the creatures on display in your zoos.'

'That's true,' Stephen had to agree.

A suspicious thought came to the Tibetan. 'Do you wish to put the Meh-teh in a cage?'

'No,' Stephen shook his head vigorously. 'We don't want to put *anything* in a cage.'

The Tibetan patted the head of the nearest yak, and the animal returned the affection by leaning closer to him. 'That is wise,' the Tibetan said. 'Cages cannot hold the Meh-teh.'

Wind whipped more snow in at them, and Stephen decided to push the conversation forward. 'Can you tell us where Professor Marchwood went?'

'And what route he took?' Mike added.

The Tibetan twisted and pointed straight through the village before jerking his hand away to the side. 'There is a path leading from the north of the village. It is steep but it has many good ledges for explorers to use as a camp.'

'And Marchwood went that way?' Stephen asked.

'Yes.'

'Thank you,' Stephen said, giving a yak a friendly rub on the forehead.

'Yeah,' Mike nodded, 'we appreciate it.'

The Tibetan gave a pleasant little bow. 'Travel safely,' he said before beginning to lead his animals away.

'Come on,' Stephen said, leading Mike through the village. 'This way.'

Mike hurried to keep up. 'I'd appreciate it more if we didn't have to climb that path.'

'It's fine,' Stephen said placatingly.

The far end of the village was marked by a change in conditions underfoot, with far more frozen ground waiting ahead. 'That's ice, that is,' Mike grumbled. 'It's not even snow.'

'Diddums,' Stephen laughed without any sympathy. 'We'll make a snowman on the way back.'

'Dunno about that,' Mike laughed, 'but I wouldn't mind taking a few snowballs back to hit John with for making us walk up this mountain.'

Stephen began the long yomp up the mountain. 'Come on.'

The two guards half-carried the near unconscious Elizabeth back through the series of stone tunnels to her cell.

Though her eyes seemed to be almost closed, Elizabeth was not as unconscious as she pretended to be. Her brain was entirely alert and her collapse during the interrogation had been an act. The questioning and the pain that had been inflicted for refusing to answer had been awful, but she had never lost control or passed out as she had pretended to.

On the way back, Elizabeth kept her eyes open just enough to see the various doors she passed and to begin forming a mental picture of this complex of tunnels. There were a number of the modern airlock style doors but most of the passages seemed to have something more basic, like wooden doors, leading off of them.

The one thing that startled Elizabeth – almost enough to break out of her performance of being semi-conscious – was a large doorway that had heavy, reinforced, metal doors. These riveted doors hung wide open on foot-long hinges, showing a huge pile of dirty white fur gathered in the corner of the room in a ball. She wasn't sure if it was the mass moulting of an animal, or actually the animal itself, as she was dragged by too quickly.

A moment after she was past the doorway, Elizabeth heard a chorus of agonised screams and roars from that room. Something in there was suffering terribly. Despite her concern for whatever was in pain back there, she remained limp, carefully taking in and remembering each door she passed until she was dragged into her cell and dumped none-too-gently on her bed.

She waited, unmoving on the uncomfortable mattress, until the door was closed. She listened as the metal latch was dropped on the outside of the door, leaving her alone in the cell.

Quietly, she slid off the bed and hurried to the door. She peered out of the small window. Once she was sure that the corridor was empty, she sat on the bed and started unlacing her boot.

Professor Marchwood opened the door to his guest just a few moments after the knock had sounded. 'Ah, John,' he beamed. 'Come in, please.'

John entered the neat little office and shook Marchwood's outstretched hand. 'Thank you for agreeing to see me so quickly.'

'Your assistant was quite insistent.' The professor sounded rather disapproving about that.

John smiled wryly and accepted the seat Marchwood indicated for him to sit in. He straightened his suit and hoped he didn't look as uncomfortable as he felt. 'I don't think TIM would appreciate being called my assistant but yes, he is rather persuasive.'

'Thank you, John,' TIM's voice said in John's mind.

'You didn't mention last night that you are a journalist,' the professor said. There was a definite hint of accusation in there, and real distaste for journalists. That would be understandable, given how many of them had made a laughingstock of Marchwood in the past.

'Didn't I say?' John asked, innocently.

'No,' Marchwood replied bluntly.

'I'm sorry about that,' John said as sincerely as he could.

The professor glanced down at the notes on a pad on his desk. 'Your credentials are certainly very impressive, particularly for one so young.'

'The paper likes us to sound good,' John said easily. 'Whether I live up to it all is another matter.'

'I'm sure you will, John,' Marchwood said.

'Thank you,' John nodded graciously before deliberately flitting the thought *Now I would really appreciate a cup of tea* through his mind.

'Can I offer you tea?' Professor Marchwood suggested.

Well, that answered one question. 'That would be excellent, thank you,' John replied with a thin smile.

Marchwood pressed a button on the intercom on his desk. 'Baines, could we have some refreshments, please? A pot of tea.'

'Lovely,' John smiled.

Marchwood leaned forward conspiratorially. 'There will be biscuits as well.'

'Even better,' John answered.

Professor Marchwood looked at John curiously. 'How do you plan to record our conversation?' he asked.

John had prepared his cover. 'Oh, I have a notepad,' he said, plucking a small pad and a biro from his pockets.

Marchwood seemed rather disappointed. 'Not one of those little personal tape recorders?'

'I'm afraid they're saved for people much further up the food chain than me,' John explained self-depreciatingly.

'Oh, I bet you're far more advanced than you're letting on,' the professor answered.

There was no doubting the sting in that statement.

John met it head on. 'I rather think a lot of us are, Professor,' he said evenly.

Marchwood was not ready to be so candid. 'Why do you say that?'

'Something you said last night.' John settled into his chair and looked the professor directly in the eyes. 'That it's rather arrogant to assume that humanity has reached the zenith of its evolution, don't you think?'

'Oh, I agree,' Marchwood said quickly. 'I do think that.'

John pressed on. 'So how do you think man will evolve next?'

'You saw that in the exhibition,' Marchwood replied.

'I saw *something* in the exhibition,' John countered. 'Something that didn't look like it belonged here.'

'Would a Neanderthal Man look like he belonged here?' Marchwood retorted.

John pulled a deep breath. 'Professor, you and I both know we're fencing with words here.' He kept going, to stop Marchwood from interrupting. 'I think it's time for some plain speaking.'

'I quite agree,' Marchwood said. 'Say what's on your mind.'

The presence of the word "mind" was clearly not an accident either. John continued to push at Marchwood. 'I think you suggested that mankind's next evolution would be developing abilities with the mind because you have already developed some of those powers yourself.'

'That would be absurd,' Marchwood said, but he didn't deny the accusation and couldn't hide the amused twinkle in his eye.

'Unless it was true,' John said evenly. 'And this exhibition is your way of reaching out to anyone else who might have gone through a similar experience.'

'And what makes you think something so unlikely?' Marchwood asked. He sounded almost playful. 'You can't have any real clue about it... unless you have some of those abilities too.'

The way Marchwood acted had put John on edge. 'Or a very suspicious mind,' he said.

'Suspicious minds are a terrible thing,' the professor said.

John decided to end the games. 'Professor, are you more evolved than the average human?'

'Do I seem more advanced?'

'A straight answer, please, Professor,' John said sharply.

Marchwood also adopted a sharper tone. 'Wouldn't those require straight questions?' The door opened and Baines entered carrying a tray. 'Ah, here's the tea.'

'So it is,' John said.

'Milk and sugar?' Baines asked blandly, apparently unaware of the tense atmosphere he had walked into.

'Just milk, please,' John answered.

As he reached out a hand to take the cup and saucer from Baines, John was hit with a wave of nausea. The cup ratted in the saucer as his hand shook.

'Are you all right?' Now it was Baines who sounded amused.

'Just a head...' John struggled to focus his thoughts. 'Just a headache.'

He couldn't concentrate.

He tried to jaunt.

He tried to contact TIM.

He couldn't control his mind.

His body wouldn't do anything he tried to make it do.

The cup and saucer crashed to the floor.

Stephen and Mike had made their way up the steep path using a mixture of walking and jaunting. They were careful about using their ability to teleport but, in a few instances, it was the only way to make any progress.

After a long and painfully slow ascent, they finally found themselves on a small, shielded plateau, protected from the wind by snowdrifts and large jutting rocks. Those same rocks took the brunt of any snow that was blowing at the mountainside, making this a perfect spot for a climber to camp.

Despite this, the ground was still covered with a blanket of snow several inches deep. However, it was obvious from the artificial shapes of the undulations in the snow that there was something under the wintry covering.

'This doesn't look natural at all,' Stephen said.

Mike experimentally scraped away the top few inches of snow on a drift. 'I agree with you. What do you think? Is this Marchwood's camp?'

'Could be,' Stephen shrugged. 'We can't tell with all this snow on it though.'

Mike brushed the snow from his gloved hands. 'Better get rid of it, then.'

Combining their minds, Stephen and Mike focused on carefully lifting the snow from the ground.

The flakes rose slowly at first, moving to the side of the ledge where they dropped onto the top of a drift. But those initial few flakes soon became a blizzard of snow rising from the ground and sweeping through the air to increase the size of the drift. Inch after inch of the covering was removed, slowly revealing what had long been buried underneath. Firstly, it was the highest point of a tent and then, secondly, its canvas sides. As the entire surface of the tent appeared, so did the scattered remnants of the camp. A circle of stones had been home to a fire, around that were boxes of supplies and a few rucksacks.

Wind and the moving snow had caused notebooks and charts to begin spilling from the backpacks, while tinned food had begun to fall through the broken side of a crate before becoming trapped in a drift of snow. Last to emerge from the frozen covering were two rifles, both had been smashed quite deliberately. The stocks were shattered, and the long metal barrels were bent into almost comical U-shapes.

Mike carefully picked up one of the rifles and looked at the broken weapon with disdain. 'Somebody hates guns as much as we do,' he said.

Stephen nodded slowly, his eyes looking nervously out over the mountains as the cold wind began to blow in a fresh flurry of snow. 'But what can do *that* to a gun?'

After ensuring that the corridor outside of her cell was quiet and empty, Elizabeth had turned her boot lace into a loop and then lowered the hooped end through the window. After swinging it back and forth a few times, she felt the lace catch on something. Pulling the lace upwards she heard the latch on the outside of the door scrape upwards and, a moment later, she pulled the door open.

After quickly lacing her boot again, Elizabeth slipped out into the corridor.

Professor Marchwood tilted his head in feigned concern. 'Are you ill, John? Is something wrong?'

John tried again to reach out to the Lab. 'TIM… TIM…'

There was no reply, just that terrible heavy crushing pain in his head. He tried reaching for his belt, but he could barely move his arms.

'John?' Professor Marchwood's voice suddenly seemed very far away.

'I… I think I should… I need to…'

'Leave?' Professor Marchwood offered helpfully.

'Need to leave,' John slurred.

'If you must,' Baines said. He pointed a taunting finger at the exit. 'The door's just there…'

John pulled his energy and concentration together. He managed to struggle to his feet before his legs buckled and he toppled to the floor.

'…if you can reach it,' Baines smirked maliciously.

In the Lab, TIM's lights pulsed as he tried to reach out to the museum. 'John? John, can you hear me?'

Elizabeth had carefully closed her cell door before quickly retying her boot lace. She crept along the corridor, listening intently for any sign of movement. She tried reaching out with her mind to John or to TIM but whatever force had dampened her abilities earlier was still affecting her. Her abilities were completely suppressed.

She cautiously picked her way along the corridor, recognising the doors she had been dragged past. She tried to peer inside and found the metal doors all locked or sealed. She kept moving until she reached the wide doorway to the room that had contained the mass of white fur. She wondered what they could have been. Was it possible that another alien race was on Earth and was being held captive in that room?

Peering inside the room, Elizabeth was struck by the slightly stale smell which was a bit like that of a wet dog.

The room, however, was empty. The hairy creatures had gone.

The wind had picked up again on the mountainside at the wrecked camp. Stephen and Mike sifted through the remains, searching for clues.

Abruptly, Mike straightened, tilting his head to keep his ear out of the wind. 'Did you hear something?' he asked.

Stephen lifted the flap of a tent and peered inside. 'Like what?'

Mike shook his head, trying to focus on the indistinct sound. 'I'm not sure? Something moving in the snow, maybe?'

'You're getting paranoid, you are,' Stephen said, reaching into the tent to pull out a rucksack. 'What would anybody be doing up here?'

'Stephen…' Mike sounded worried.

Stephen was still looking inside the tent. 'I mean we're miles from anywhere. There's nobody around here.'

'Have you told *them* that?' Mike asked in a hollow voice.

Mike's tone made Stephen turn. All around the camp, rising from behind snow drifts, were huge creatures. They stood at least eight feet tall, were covered in shaggy off-white fur, and they were roughly the shape of a man with two arms and two legs. Set into their heads were two unsettlingly human-looking eyes, full of sadness and anger.

'I don't believe it,' Stephen breathed. 'The Yeti.'

3: Distant Relations

Mike and Stephen stared in shock and horror at the six, huge, shaggy figures surrounding them.

'I don't believe it,' Mike said. 'The Yeti – they're real.'

Stephen reached for his jaunting belt. 'Quick, Mike. Jaunt.'

Mike did as he was instructed, reaching for his own belt, but even as he tried to focus his mind on the Lab he knew that nothing was happening. 'I can't.'

'Neither can I!' Stephen gasped.

Mike looked around desperately, hoping to see some way to escape. Instead, the Yeti just continued clambering over the drifts. 'Something's dampening our powers.'

'Same as in the museum,' Stephen said, 'only much stronger this time.' One of the Yeti pulled back its lip, showing sharp, yellowing teeth. 'Run!'

'There's loads of them,' Mike cried. 'They're everywhere.' He made a move towards the largest gap between two of the Yeti, but the giants moved quickly to close the break.

'And they move faster than us,' Stephen said. A thought came to him, something in the way the Yeti had moved to cover their escape…

He leaped quickly towards the widest gap still between two Yeti. They moved as he expected them to, closing that gap, and he took another step in that direction, making them close the distance even further – but as they did so, they left a gap further round the camp he and Mike could make a bolt for.

'There's a gap!' Stephen yelled. 'Run for it!'

He sprinted across the slippery ground but stopped as he heard a terrible CRACK and a yell from behind him. Turning round he saw Mike lying on the ground, his legs under a drift of snow and ice that had been knocked loose by a Yeti's movement.

'Mike!'

The younger man struggled against the weight on his legs but with no success. 'I can't move.'

'Come on!' Stephen urged.

But it was no use. Mike couldn't get his legs free. 'I can't get out. It's too heavy.'

The Yeti were moving closer to Stephen, but he couldn't bring himself to leave Mike behind. 'Try!'

Mike saw the Yeti closing on Stephen. 'Go! Get out of here!'

'I can't just leave you,' Stephen protested.

But a Yeti was already standing over Mike. It reached down and grabbed his shoulder in one huge hand. 'Go for help!' Mike pleaded. 'Go!'

The Yeti were almost on top of Stephen. 'All right,' he called. 'I'll be back as quick as I can.'

Stephen ran the last few steps to the edge of the camp and threw himself over the drift of snow.

'Run!' Mike shouted. 'Go! Go!'

Stephen flew over the drift, expecting to land on the snow beyond. Instead, he found himself sailing through the air for a good second longer than expected. He had leaped over the drift at a point where the rock face dropped away most steeply. He landed hard on a frozen face of ice that was covered with a thin layer of snow. He skidded forward on his stomach, sliding fast and out of control on the steep slope, until he came to an ungainly stop a hundred yards down, when he slammed into another drift of snow.

Pulling himself together, Stephen scrambled to his feet. He was winded but unscathed. The Yeti hadn't followed him down the slope, but they were making their way onto the path. He picked himself up and made his way through the deep snow, until he was on the path himself.

He reached out mentally, trying to contact the Lab.

He was still being blocked.

The Yeti were lumbering down the path behind him, closing the gap at an alarming rate.

Stephen hurried down the path as fast as he could.

Mike looked up at the Yeti gripping his shoulder and offered the friendliest grin he could muster. The giant creature simply looked at him, and Mike found himself deeply disturbed by the very human mix of emotions in its eyes. He only broke eye contact with it when another Yeti grabbed his other shoulder.

Two of the Yeti ripped the heavy covering of snow and ice away, releasing Mike's legs. The other two Yeti hauled him up to his feet.

Mike tried to raise his arms above his head. 'I hope you lot realise this means I've surrendered.'

The two Yeti yanked him forward and he struggled to move his legs, numb from being trapped under the weight of the freezing snow and ice.

A moment later he was being dragged away into the mountains.

Baines and Professor Marchwood looked at the pained figure of John as he twitched on the floor.

'Well, this proves we're right,' Baines said.

'Oh, yes. He's definitely a telepath,' Marchwood agreed.

Baines looked disgusted that Marchwood had wasted time saying something so plainly apparent. 'Obviously.'

'He's in so much pain,' Marchwood said.

'Isn't he.' Baines said with satisfaction.

'Is there any need to prolong the attack on him this way?' Marchwood objected. 'It's cruel.'

Baines looked at Marchwood with disgust. 'It's making a point.'

'To whom?' Marchwood challenged.

'To *you*, if nobody else,' Baines barked sharply. 'There is no room for weakness in our work.'

Marchwood was still focused on John. The young telepath was bringing his movements under control. He had started to crawl towards the door.

'He's fighting it,' the professor said in amazement.

'So he is,' Baines agreed. He drew a small box from his pocket and looked at its screen.

Marchwood peered over Baines's shoulder at the box's screen. 'He's trying to order his thoughts. It's very impressive.'

'It is, isn't it?' Baines said with distaste. 'Well, let's really give him a challenge, shall we?'

'No, Baines, that's just cruel.' Marchwood tried to take the control box from his so-called assistant, but Baines pushed him away viciously.

'It's *necessary*,' he snarled, and operated a control on the side of the box.

John's mind screamed.

Stephen tried once more to jaunt back to the Lab, but his abilities were still dulled. Looking back over his shoulder he saw the two giant off-white Yeti lumbering through the snow after him. They were better suited to walking through snow than he was, with long muscular legs which could step over the top of the deep drifts, while Stephen had to push his way through the snow. He had no doubt that they would catch him within a few minutes.

Looking around, Stephen saw a gleaming strip to the side of an overhanging snowy face. It looked like ice. That wall of snow faced the sun and it seemed clear to him that some of the snow had melted at a rare point when it had been warm enough, dripping down to the flat level below only to turn back into ice as the temperature dropped again. The glistening strip of ice ran downhill as far as Stephen could see.

Stephen pushed his way through the snow, forcing his way towards the strip of ice. He could hear the Yeti getting closer. He heard their heavy steps kicking snow aside, he heard their breathing as they pulled in huge mouthfuls of air.

Closer.

They were getting closer.

Only a few feet to the ice.

They were even closer.

The snow thrown up by the Yeti's running landed in the drift to his side. They could only be a few feet behind him. With those long arms they would catch him in seconds.

He had to keep moving.

Yeti fingertips clawed at his coat.

The contact gave Stephen the burst of energy to take the last few feet to the ice in one great leap.

He landed on the ice and instantly began to skid away down the mountain like a child on a slide. He jerked his head round to look back, terrified he would see the Yeti following him, but the great ape-men had only taken a few steps after him before something had stopped them. They stared at him with sad, almost human, eyes. Then turned away and started back up the mountain.

Stephen turned his eyes back to the ice ahead.

The slide down the mountain was steeper and far more terrifying than Stephen had expected. The icy face of the snow-covered rocks raced by, just a few precious inches to his side. If he caught any of the sharp black struts of rock jutting out, they would certainly tear his skin or shatter a bone. The slope steepened and his pace increased.

'Stephen? Mike?' a familiar – and incredibly welcome – voice sounded in his mind.

'TIM?' he exclaimed in relief.

An instant after hearing TIM's familiar voice in his thoughts, Stephen jaunted, and a moment later was sitting on his backside on the jaunting pad in the Lab. Momentum from the icy slide sent him skidding from one side of the pad to the other.

Elizabeth hadn't stayed long in the empty cell. Whatever had been in there would probably be brought back before long and she had no intention of being there when they returned.

Slipping back out into the corridor, Elizabeth made her way along the stone passage, staying carefully to the shadows. The doors she encountered remained resolutely closed until she found one that was left ajar.

Peering inside, she saw a dark room full of vertical canisters – each standing about seven feet tall. The walls were lined with these containers, running into the shadows of what looked like a very long room.

Elizabeth crept inside and looked around, making sure she was alone. She couldn't see anyone and all she could hear was the dull hum of these machines.

The nearest seven canisters – four on one side and three on the other – had a single circular window on the front that was illuminated by a dull, bluish light from within. Inside the nearest one, Elizabeth saw a teenage girl who appeared to be wearing 1960s era clothes that had a rather French fashion.

A boy of a similar age was in the next canister. From his clothes she guessed he was from India, even further back than the 1960s. In each of the seven canisters she found a teenager, all from different parts of the world and, judging by their clothes, from varying points in the past seventy or eighty years. They seemed to be in some kind of deep sleep or coma.

There were controls by the side of each of the canisters and a larger control panel against the wall by the door, but Elizabeth simply couldn't make head nor tail of them. The dials and meters were marked in a language she didn't recognise, and in letters which looked alien. She could have guessed at the purpose of one of two of the controls but didn't dare risk the lives of the children frozen inside.

There was nothing she could do for these captives without some help, so Elizabeth carefully made her way back into the corridor and left the door exactly as she had found it.

She made her way along the corridor, dipping quickly into the shadows of a doorway as she heard a guard approach. She let him pass before continuing.

About twenty yards further on, the corridor took a sharp left-hand turn. On the left side of the corridor were banks of equipment which fed through the wall ahead into whatever was beyond the doorway that now barred her way.

She heard a clicking from the door and quickly pressed herself into the narrow gap between two of the banks of machinery. She moved just in time to avoid being seen by the guard who walked past her hiding place obliviously. She watched him turn the corner and disappear from view, before hurrying to the door he had come through, catching it just before it closed. She held it open just a fraction and listened to what was being said inside.

'The human telepath is resisting the suppression field.'

That was Baines's voice, but it sounded like it was coming from a speaker of some sort.

Baines's voice sounded again. 'Relay more power to us.'

There was a dull click and Elizabeth assumed that was the speaker or transmitter – or whatever it was – being switched off.

Another voice came, this time definitely from inside the room. 'Baines wants *another* increase in power?'

Elizabeth risked peering inside and saw John's face on a screen. It was twisted and contorted with agony. He was being tortured. A number of men, in the same uniforms as the guards who had dumped her in her cell, were hunched over a series of control panels.

'Increase power,' one of them said.

Elizabeth had to fight against her instinct to run into the room and somehow try to stop John's torture. Without her powers she would be outnumbered and captured within seconds, and that would do nothing to help him.

The computers and machines in the corridor were somehow linked to this control room.

Closing the door, Elizabeth did what she could to scramble the lock, then returned to the machines and began ripping a panel free. Inside were wires and glowing circuits. She tore the innards of the machine out and moved on to the next panel, yanking cables from their connections and pulling boards of circuits from their housing. Immediately the lights flickered, and she heard a commotion from the control room. The men inside were panicking.

It sounded as if she had succeeded.

Realising there was nothing more she could do, Elizabeth ran.

Baines shook his control box as it gave an unhealthy crackling sound.

'What's happening?' Marchwood asked.

Baines tried again to reset the box in his hand. Nothing happened. He shook it in frustration. 'The control is dead.'

'Can't you get it back?' Marchwood asked.

Baines reacted as if it was the stupidest question he could have been asked. 'Don't you think I would if I could?'

'Is there another way to contact them?' Marchwood asked.

Lying on the floor, John's mind had slowly begun to clear. He forced his thoughts into order, forced his mind to do as he instructed. He concentrated with all his might. 'TIM? Can you hear me? TIM?'

Stephen was already talking fast as he hurried from the jaunting pad to the table at the heart of the Lab. 'The Yeti got Mike and…'

But TIM cut him off abruptly. 'That will have to wait, Stephen.'

'But Mike's in danger.'

'So is John,' TIM replied. 'I have lost contact with him. I can only just make out his thoughts.'

Stephen's attitude instantly changed to concern for his other friend. 'Where is he?' he asked. 'At the museum?'

'Yes,' TIM confirmed.

'I'll go and get him,' Stephen said, turning back towards the jaunting pad.

But TIM's voice held him back. 'No.'

'What?'

'Not yet,' TIM corrected himself.

Two new jaunting belts, looking exactly the same as the one Stephen was currently wearing, appeared on the table.

'Change your jaunting belt,' TIM said, 'and take this one for John.'

Stephen quickly swapped belts. 'What's different?'

'I have updated them to block out most of the dampening effect which nullifies your powers,' TIM said, sounding as close to proud of his achievements as a computer could be. 'I wish I had completed them sooner.'

'Right,' Stephen said. He would save his congratulations for later.

TIM wasn't quite finished. 'One other thing, Stephen.'

'What's that?' Stephen asked.

'Take a stun gun.'

Baines was becoming increasingly frustrated.

'I can't contact base!' His voice rose in irritation. 'All of our power comes from there.'

Professor Marchwood hovered at Baines's elbow but was more of an irritation than of any assistance. 'What's happened there?'

'I don't know,' Baines snapped viciously.

Marchwood looked at the prone figure of John, who lay still on the floor. He seemed to be unconscious, but his pain appeared to have stopped. 'We need to do something before he recovers.'

'I'll deal with him myself, if I have to,' Baines said harshly. There was no doubting that he meant to kill their captive if necessary.

'No!' Marchwood protested. 'That's unacceptable!'

Baines sneered at Marchwood's weakness but, before he could speak, the office's door was kicked open. Stephen stepped into the doorway, a stun gun aimed at Baines and Professor Marchwood.

'Don't move, either of you!' Stephen said, with as much menace as he could muster.

'Stephen!' Baines looked at him unconcerned. 'How utterly… *expected*… to see you again.'

Stephen ignored the implied threat. 'If you speak again, I'll shoot.'

John's voice croaked from the floor. 'Stephen?'

Keeping his stun gun aimed at Baines and Marchwood, Stephen used his free hand to help John to his feet. 'Come on. You're getting out of here.'

John swayed woozily and staggered a half step backwards towards the door. 'Just give me a minute.'

'I'm not sure we've got that long,' Stephen replied.

John lurched out of the door, using the frame to stay upright. 'Come on then.'

Stephen waited until John was outside and then waved his gun at his captives. 'If you follow us, you know what you'll get.'

He didn't wait for an answer, stepping backwards into the corridor and slamming the door shut hard behind him.

John seemed to be recovering and looked almost amused by Stephen's show of bravado. *'If you follow us, you know what you'll get?* Have you been watching bad gangster movies again?'

Stephen shrugged. 'I had to make some kind of threat, didn't I?' He pulled the new jaunting belt from inside his jacket and handed it to his friend. 'Put this on.'

John took the belt and looked at it in confusion. 'I've already got one.'

'TIM's been busy redesigning them to block the interference,' Stephen explained.

'Has he?' John quickly put the belt around his waist. 'Let's go.'

The two Tomorrow People faded away.

'John!' TIM's relieved voice greeted John as he arrived on the jaunting pad. 'You're safe.'

'Thanks to you and Stephen here.' John said, making his way to a seat and dropping gratefully into it. He pulled off his obsolete belt and Stephen took it from him, dropping it onto the table. It disappeared a few seconds later.

TIM explained his work on the belts. 'I analysed the interference I detected in your thoughts when you were at the museum and was able to build protection from it into the belts.'

'That's clever of you,' John said appreciatively, accepting a glass of fruit juice from Stephen.

'I thought so,' TIM replied.

John couldn't help smiling. 'Modest as ever, TIM.'

TIM continued, beginning to relish his explanation. 'The analysis showed that this is a very focused and projected form of interference.'

'Yes, I've felt it,' John said, rubbing at his temple. 'Can't say I cared for it much.'

Stephen's lips pursed in thought. 'It's focused and directed, so…'

'…it is not a natural phenomenon,' TIM confirmed.

'I think we had all guessed that already,' John said slowly. 'No, it's an attack.' He paused to pick his words carefully. 'A direct attack on the Tomorrow People. An attack on *us*.'

The control room door was finally prised open and the technicians Elizabeth had seen operating the various devices managed to force their way out into the corridor outside. They stared in shock at the damage Elizabeth had inflicted on their banks of machinery.

'It's sabotage!' the leading technician said.

The man at his shoulder agreed. 'There must be an enemy inside the complex.'

There didn't seem to be any other logical explanation for what had happened. 'Check the prisoners and secure the base.'

Elizabeth heard the wail of what-could-only-be an alarm and she knew that her handiwork had been discovered. It would only be a matter of minutes before they found her cell was empty.

There were no markings to help her work out a way to an exit, but instinct told her that the further away from the control room she got, the closer she would be to a way out. Sure enough, the doors were rougher, simpler and less frequent as she moved into what seemed like a more primitive part of the tunnel complex. The floor became as rough as the walls and the ceiling began to slope upwards. She followed the tunnel up until she felt a chill breeze begin to drift along the passage, which darkened as the lights gradually were becoming more spaced out.

And then... Elizabeth's escape seemed to be over. The passage stopped abruptly at a roughly hewn rocky wall. And yet, somehow, she still felt the wind coming from the wall. No, it was coming *through* the wall. Tentatively, she reached her hand towards the rock... and her hand passed through it as it wasn't there. She understood immediately that was because the wall itself wasn't there. It was some sort of holographic projection. The only way to find out what was on the other side was to go through it, so Elizabeth took a deep breath and stepped forward...

...and found herself in the same passage, only it was more brightly lit, with the illumination coming from an opening in the wall just ahead.

Elizabeth ran towards the opening and found herself stepping out onto a ledge, high in a range of snowy mountains. Given the size, and violently jutting shapes of the peaks, she was sure it had to be the Himalayas. She shivered as the cold hit her. She was dressed for London, not for Tibetan mountains. The only way she was going to get back to London was to get away from whatever was dampening her powers and then to jaunt home.

The ledge Elizabeth had emerged onto snaked down the mountain, winding round an icy rock face. Elizabeth's own face was stung by the snow and ice blown by the freezing wind, but she forced herself to move. She had to get away from this area. Her feet slid on the icy, uneven surface but she concentrated on making good time away from the opening to the caves. Soon, she had rounded the curve, and the cave was out of sight. She kept going until she could hear something in the distance. Over the sound of the wind, she could hear a rough, guttural sound.

It was the breathing of an animal.

The path she was following was lined with any number of protruding shards of rock and she quickly hurried into the cover of the largest she could see. A minute later she saw something she would have thought impossible a few days earlier. Creatures standing eight feet tall, that were neither apes nor men but also somehow managed to be both, moved up the path. Covered in a thick off-white fur, these were the creatures she assumed had been held in the cell when she'd briefly seen one of them curled into a ball, and then heard their frightened screams of pain.

She was certain that these were the legendary Abominable Snowmen of the Himalayas, the Yeti.

Even more impossibly, they were half dragging, half pushing the reluctant figure of Mike.

In the Lab, John sat wearily at the main table, gratefully drinking a cup of strong tea which TIM had supplied.

'Just what I needed. Thank you, TIM.'

TIM disagreed, the coloured lights above the table pulsing as he spoke. 'What you need is rest, John.'

John refused to accept the guidance. His first instinct was to rescue his lost friends. 'I'll think about that after we've rescued Mike from...' he paused. 'Are you really sure they were...' He shook his head, struggling to believe the words about to come out of his mouth. 'I can hardly bring myself to say it.'

Stephen saved John from his ordeal. 'The Abominable Snowmen,' he supplied.

'Yes,' John said ruefully. 'Them.' He still sounded sceptical about the story Stephen had related about what had happened in the Himalayas.

'They were real enough,' Stephen said firmly.

'Big, huge and hairy.' He thought for a moment, recalling those unexpectedly human faces. 'There was something about them, though.'

'Like what?' John asked.

'Like they were intelligent,' Stephen said slowly. 'You could see it in their eyes. It was like they had… I don't know… a soul?'

John gave the younger man a sour look. 'Don't go metaphysical on us.'

Stephen replied quickly, without backing down. 'I'm only saying they weren't just big stupid animals. They're more than that. Intelligent.'

John's cynicism faded. 'That's interesting.'

'It's why I didn't argue when TIM told me to rescue you first, John. I sort of knew they wouldn't kill Mike, just capture him.

'I hope you're right.' John muttered.

'Do you think these Yeti are aliens?' Stephen asked, excitedly.

'I don't know.' John sighed wearily. 'The truth is, I don't know *what* to think. My brain still feels like it's been put through a mincing machine.' That was certainly true. He still felt dizzy and nauseous from Baines's attack.

TIM's lights pulsed again as he spoke. 'What do you remember about the attack on your mind, John?'

'Only that I'd rather never go through it again,' John answered honestly.

'The revised jaunting belts should ensure that is much less likely,' TIM said. 'It would be easier to analyse the attack if you could describe it.'

John took a welcome sip of tea. 'Maybe I can share it with you?'

'Is that wise?' Stephen asked.

John frowned. 'How do you mean?'

'After the damage it did to you, what if it hits TIM the same way?' Stephen explained.

'Thank you for your concern, Stephen,' TIM's voice rumbled, 'but this would only be the memory of the attack, an echo of it, if you like. It will not hurt me.'

Stephen wasn't convinced. 'Are you positive about that?'

'Quite sure,' TIM replied confidently. 'I am concerned for *you*, though, John. I do think you should rest before you revisit this experience.'

John shook his head stubbornly. 'No, TIM. Elizabeth and Mike are missing. We can worry about me after we get them back.'

'Very well,' TIM conceded reluctantly, 'but I will monitor your health and if I sense that you are in distress, I shall end the contact.'

'That sounds fair,' Stephen told John.

'Sounds like I'm being bullied,' John grumbled.

Once more, Stephen didn't back down. 'Sometimes even *you* need to be told what to do – and Elizabeth's not here to do it, so we're having a go!'

Realising that he was not going to win this argument, John conceded and looked upwards at the glowing lights above the table. It was a habit everyone had fallen into ever since the Lab and TIM had been built. 'Are you ready, TIM?'

'I am prepared,' the computer assured him.

After placing his hands palm down on the table, John glanced at Stephen. 'There's no need for you to join this, Stephen. In fact, it's probably better if one of us keeps a completely clear head.'

That made sense. 'All right.'

'Are you ready, John?' asked TIM.

'Honestly, I'm not sure,' John answered tersely, 'but let's get on with it.'

The lights over the table dimmed to a soothing turquoise. 'Relax your mind, John, and let me connect with your memories.'

John tried to drain the stress and anxiety from his mind, to open it up to TIM. But as he tried, memories of the desperately empty feeling of having no powers came back. It jarred his mind and, alongside that horrible devoid feeling, the memories of the pain came suddenly. Instinctively, he pushed back against it.

'Your mind is reacting reflexively,' TIM said in a soothing voice, 'withdrawing from experiencing the pain again.'

Taking a deep, ragged breath, John tried again, imposing order and discipline on his thoughts. 'Don't worry. I can do it.'

'Try to distance yourself from the memories,' TIM urged, 'as if you are looking into someone's mind.'

'That's easier said than done,' John answered tersely.

'I will help you, John,' TIM reassured him.

John focused himself again. 'I'll try.'

'Use me as an anchor for your mind, John.'

John shifted uncomfortably in his seat. 'It's so difficult not to react.'

'Focus,' TIM urged. 'Stay focused.'

Inside his mind, John stepped backwards from the immediacy of his memories and began to view them dispassionately. He recognised the pain he had endured but he was distanced enough from it that he was unaffected. 'There,' he said with satisfaction.

'I think I have it. Can you read those thoughts, TIM?'

'I can,' TIM replied immediately. 'I am recording what I sense from you.'

The memories began to edge closer to the front of John's mind, threatening to bring back the pain and disorientation. He pushed back against them, holding them at bay. 'I'll keep going as long as I can.'

'Just a little longer,' TIM urged.

John winced as he began to feel nauseous again. 'It's so difficult.' He strengthened his defences and held firm.

After an eternity, TIM finally ended the torment. 'That is enough, John,' he said. 'I have drawn enough from your memories.'

John immediately pushed those memories into the deepest recesses of his mind. With TIM's aid, he was successful. 'Thank goodness for that,' he breathed in relief.

Stephen was by his side, concerned. 'Are you okay?'

'As okay as I can be, I think,' John nodded.

'Is he, TIM?'

TIM took a moment to consider the question. 'Physically, yes,' he said, but added, 'Mentally, it may take some time to fully recover.'

'We don't *have* time for that,' John said firmly.

'It will take me a short while to analyse the information you gave me,' TIM said carefully.

John heaved himself up onto his feet. 'Then we should go and find Mike.'

Stephen put a hand on John's shoulder and pushed him back into a sitting position. 'Maybe we'll do that when you can stand up properly.'

TIM interrupted gently. 'This will take thirty minutes,' he said. 'John, I suggest that you use that time for some induced sleep.'

John looked set to protest but then his shoulders slumped. 'I don't think I've got the energy to argue.'

'I will wake you when I am finished,' TIM assured him. John wearily made his way to a couch and lay down.

'I'll try to contact Mike and Elizabeth,' Stephen said, 'though I'm sure they'd have been in touch with us if they were able to.'

Elizabeth had been in two minds as she saw Mike being dragged away by the Yeti. Her immediate instinct was to follow and try to set her friend free, but good sense held her back. The damage she had caused in the complex would lead to her escape being discovered before long and the tunnels would be full of guards searching for her. The only way she could help Mike now was to get away and try to contact John or TIM in the Lab.

The cold and the wind cut through Elizabeth's clothing, chilling her to the bone, but she kept moving. The clouds were growing a darker, more ominous grey and the leading edge of what looked like it would be a heavy fall of snow began to land on her. She ignored it and kept moving.

The path continued to wind unevenly down the mountain and Elizabeth followed it, picking her way carefully over the increasingly slippery ground.

After a few minutes she reached a plateau with the remnants of a climbers' camp on it. Just for a second, she considered taking shelter from the increasingly bitter wind in the tent, but she knew she had to move on. However, she did rummage through the rucksacks and found a heavy woollen sweater which she quickly pulled on over her coat.

She heard movement. Something was coming closer. Through the loud gusts of wind, she could hear the regular sound of feet scrunching in snow and a heavy animalistic breathing.

Yeti.

She recognised the source of the sound, just in time to dip out of sight behind a drift of snow. Sure enough, a few seconds later, two Yeti made their way up a path onto the plateau.

The shaggy giants stopped and looked around the camp site. Elizabeth wondered if they had seen her, but she was sure that she had found her way into the cover of the snow drift before the Yeti had reached the little ledge.

But something was troubling the Yeti.

One of the Yeti turned its gaze to the backpacks that Elizabeth had rummaged through.

Elizabeth understood what had caught their attention. She had cast the rucksacks aside rather than put them back exactly as she had found them. The Yeti knew something had changed at the camp. It wouldn't take long for them to work out that the backpacks had been moved.

Moving as carefully and as quietly as she could, Elizabeth slid away from the snow drift, easing her way down the incline until she would be able to make her way onto the path.

Mike had been hauled up the rough mountain path by the four giant Yeti. He had tried to communicate with them, to show that he had peaceful intentions. They showed no sign of having understood anything. They had ignored everything that he had said and kept him in a tight grip until they led him into a cave – the same cave which none of them knew Elizabeth had recently escaped from. They pulled and pushed him along the rough tunnel until they reached what seemed to be a dead end. The Yeti kept marching towards the rough stone wall, pulling him onwards, and Mike winced, expecting to feel his face slam into the cold rock. Instead, he found himself in an extension of the corridor. Turning his head quickly he was able to see the Yeti at the back of the little group seemingly passing through a solid, stone wall.

About thirty metres past the hologram wall, the Yeti were met by three men in sinister uniforms that could only mean they were guards of some sort.

The Yeti grew immediately timid, their body language changing, with their shoulders dipping and their heads lowering as if they were trying to make themselves smaller… a smaller target, maybe?

Yes, the Yeti were terrified of these men.

Even though these giants had captured him and been none too gentle about dragging him into captivity, Mike felt a sudden sense of real sympathy for the Yeti.

While one of the guards harried the cowering Yeti away along the corridor, Mike was pushed along by the other guards until they reached a rough wooden door, which was quickly pulled open, and Mike was aggressively shoved inside.

'All right!' he protested. 'No need to push. Manners don't hurt, you know.'

By the time he had steadied himself and turned back towards his captors, the wooden door was slamming shut. Mike was about to shout something thoroughly rude when he heard the guards' voices from outside.

'She's escaped.'

'That's not possible. The door is still closed.'

'She's not in there.'

Mike held back from shouting at his captors. He had no doubt that the "she" the guards were frantically discussing was more than likely Elizabeth.

The idea that his friend had caused their captors so much difficulty lifted Mike's spirits, and he began to look around his cell, searching for a way to escape.

TIM had dimmed the lights inside the Lab to make it easier for John to fall asleep. Even though the rest had been induced and deepened by TIM's influence, dulling the lights had also helped John drift into a deep and peaceful sleep.

When he woke forty-five minutes later, John looked far more like himself.

'How do you feel, John?' TIM asked.

John offered a wry smile, amused by how much TIM sounded like a worried family doctor. 'A bit better, thanks,' he answered. 'You shouldn't have let me sleep longer than we agreed.'

TIM was not completely convinced. 'You would feel better if you rested a little longer.'

But John was not willing to countenance any further delays. 'We don't have time for that, TIM.'

A deep plastic tumbler containing a turquoise drink appeared on the table. 'This will help to balance your system,' TIM said.

'Thanks.' John took a long draw from the drink and winced at the bitter taste. 'Have you analysed whatever you managed to get out of my memories?'

'I have,' TIM replied, sounding quite enthused by his research, 'and I must say it is quite fascinating.'

'Don't keep me hanging on,' John urged the computer.

'The force which attacked your mind were actually memories themselves,' TIM explained. 'The emotions and fears of telepaths and those with psychic abilities. Their emotions are amplified and magnified, distilled into a concentrated series of mental impulses directed at susceptible minds.'

'Telepaths,' John repeated. 'It seems ironic that my memories transmitted their memories to you!'

'Yes,' TIM agreed.

'So, they are us?' Stephen was standing at the back of the room.

'It's interesting,' John said, but he sounded more than a little disappointed. 'It doesn't tell us much more than we already knew, though.'

'I am not quite finished, John,' TIM interjected.

'Carry on,' John encouraged.

'The minds they have drawn these fears from are not all from this time,' TIM continued. 'Some are from earlier times, minds not quite evolved enough to be Tomorrow People.'

Now that did interest John, a great deal. He rubbed thoughtfully at his chin. 'Would you say they are a sort of Proto-Tomorrow People, perhaps?' he mused.

'Indeed,' TIM confirmed, 'but some are a good deal more primitive. An earlier form of hominid.'

'The Yeti?' John sounded slightly surprised – or was it embarrassed – by his own question.

'Indeed.'

'So, they were telepathic after all?' Stephen mused out loud.

'Tell me, TIM,' John said, 'was Professor Marchwood's mind one of the almost-telepaths?'

'Yes,' TIM confirmed, 'I was coming to that.'

John sucked on his lower lip. 'I thought he might be.'

'He *did* pick up our thoughts,' Stephen mused.

John nodded. 'Yes, and I heard him argue with Baines about their attack on me. He was protesting at how cruel it was.' He glanced at Stephen. 'I think it's Baines who's in charge, not the professor.'

Stephen mulled that thought. 'What does all that mean?'

A resolute expression fixed itself on John's face. 'It means we're going to have another word with the professor, rather than Baines.'

Elizabeth's hands and feet were numb from the cold by the time she reached the path, but she forced herself to keep going. The ground underfoot was even more slippery than it had been higher on the mountain. She focused setting herself little targets, like the boulder twenty feet ahead or the curve in the path just beyond it. As she walked, she flexed her fingers and scrunched up her toes, trying to get some feeling back into them. It didn't work. They remained numb.

A tiredness was beginning to creep into her. She began to think about stopping, just for a moment. If she could rest just for a few minutes, maybe find a place out of the wind and snow to close her eyes and recover her energy…

No!

Elizabeth snapped her eyes open. If she sat to rest for even a minute, the cold would kill her.

Keep moving, she told herself. *Just keep moving.*

The wind dipped and she heard something.

It took a moment to realise that it came from the path behind her.

Something was following her down the path.

The Yeti were on her trail.

John stood beside Stephen on the jaunting pad, each holding a stun gun and ready to fire.

Stephen glanced back towards the lights over the central table. 'Are you sure these new belts will work?'

John answered before TIM had the chance to. 'There's only one way to find out,' he said. 'This has got to be quick.'

'Don't worry,' Stephen reassured him, 'I'm not interested in hanging around there.'

John reached for his belt. 'Right, come on.'

A second later John and Stephen reappeared back in Professor Marchwood's office, where the professor and Baines were examining a small box.

Marchwood's eyes started to widen. 'What in the…'

John and Stephen both fired their stun guns and Baines dropped silently to the floor.

Marchwood threw his hands up in terror. 'Don't kill me.'

'We don't kill people,' John snapped sourly, while Stephen pushed a jaunting belt, with a booster attached to it, into the professor's hands.

'Put this on.'

Marchwood tried to back away, shoving the belt back towards Stephen. 'I don't want to…'

The younger Tomorrow Person simply swung the belt round Marchwood and fastened it around his waist. 'I've got him.'

John focused his mind and reached for his belt. 'Let's get out of here.'

Professor Marchwood looked terrified as he appeared on the jaunting pad in the Lab.

'What is this place?' he whimpered.

'It's the Lab,' John said, taking the jaunting belt from Marchwood's waist. 'Our base if you like. More like home, really.'

TIM's voice echoed round the Lab. 'Welcome, Professor.'

Marchwood looked around the room in alarm, searching for the source of the voice. 'Who said that?'

'That's TIM,' Stephen said, leading the professor to the table in the heart of the room. 'He's… in with the bricks.'

Marchwood frowned, trying to make sense of the comment. 'Is it a computer?'

'I can answer for myself,' TIM said, sounding slightly miffed.

'Well, pardon me,' Stephen said cheekily.

TIM explained, 'I am a biotronic computer, professor.'

'I don't know what that is,' Marchwood said, simply.

'Neither do I,' Stephen admitted. 'I just accept it's TIM.'

Marchwood had been welcomed rather too warmly for John's liking. He was not going to let the academic forget that he was there to answer questions. 'Now, Professor, I think we need to know why a telepath like you is targeting other telepaths.'

Marchwood wilted under John's hard stare. 'I… It's hard to…' He chewed on his lip.

It was clear as day that Professor Marchwood was both terrified and a coward.

John chose to show no sympathy. 'And perhaps you can tell us what hold Mr Baines has on you.'

Stephen picked up the cue from John's harsh manner. 'And where he's from. How does he know about aliens?'

'Is he even from this planet himself?' John demanded.

'Please,' Marchwood whined, 'one at a time.'

'Professor,' John barked sharply, I don't think you are in any position to make demands.' He stared hard into Marchwood's eyes. 'Now tell us about Baines.'

Professor Marchwood looked for a second as if he might try to resist, but his courage crumbled and he said, 'That's not his name. I don't know what he's really called.'

John's next question followed immediately. 'Where did you meet him?'

'The Himalayas,' Marchwood answered miserably. 'He captured me there.'

'Why?' John demanded.

Stephen suggested, 'Because you're a telepath?'

'I'm not.' Marchwood shook his head vigorously, almost in fear. 'Not really. I only have some mild empathic ability, but it was just enough.'

'Just enough for what?' John pressed.

Marchwood's shoulders sank. He was almost shrinking in front of them, trying to make himself smaller, less of a target. 'Enough to catch his attention.'

John showed no sympathy. 'How?'

'Because he came to Earth to find telepaths,' Marchwood said simply.

John and Stephen exchanged a quick glance.

Stephen pressed the interrogation. 'Why?'

'His people go to inhabited planets to find telepaths,' Marchwood's voice was almost a whimper.

John was relentless. 'That still doesn't answer why.'

The explanation burst out of Marchwood. He had been pushed and frightened enough, first by Baines and then by his current captors, that he would answer whatever was asked if they would just leave him alone. 'Because they don't have any telepaths and will never produce any,' he blurted. 'They think that means other races have an unfair advantage over them, will use their abilities to attack them, so they send agents like Baines – they call them Guardians – to ensure that telepaths, empaths, anyone with psychic abilities of any sort, won't evolve on other worlds.'

'They've failed,' John said flatly. 'There are telepaths all across the galaxy.'

'Yes, they know that,' Marchwood nodded, 'however there would be many more if it wasn't for the Guardians.'

The professor's words quieted the Lab for a moment.

Stephen broke the silence after a long moment. 'Do they kill these telepaths? The Guardians, I mean.'

'No!' Marchwood sounded horrified. 'They consider themselves a civilised people. They simply put them in suspended animation – or use technology to control their minds.'

'Is that what Baines did with you?' John asked.

'No.' Marchwood looked a pitiful, crumpled sight and he sounded beaten and ashamed. 'I'm afraid I was controlled by something far simpler – my own cowardice. But he did use his technology to capture the Yeti and use them.'

'Why the Yeti?' Stephen asked curiously.

'Because they have psychic abilities,' Marchwood explained, and his natural fascination with the subject began to shine through. 'They were an offshoot of man, you see, forced into the mountains by competition from more aggressive species like the Neanderthals and, indeed, our own ancestors. They hid high up in the snows. For centuries. For millennia, really. They evolved and changed, trying to live away from mankind.'

John wasn't distracted by Marchwood's enthusiasm. 'But Baines found them,' he said, pushing the professor back on track.

Marchwood looked disappointed to be pulled away from his specialist interest. 'His equipment did,' he said, sounding rather sniffy. 'And when he did, he decided that that was the place for his Guardians to have their base on Earth.'

'How long have they been on Earth?' Stephen asked.

'And how many are there?' added John.

Marchwood gave a moment's thought. 'There are, perhaps, a dozen of them... and they've been here maybe a hundred years or so.'

'A hundred years?' Stephen processed the repercussions of that thought. 'You mean these are some of the telepaths who came before us?'[1]

'Yes,' Marchwood confirmed, 'Baines only found primitive ones, but he found them before they could really develop.'

'He got to them before they broke out.' John's eyes bored into Marchwood. 'And what did he do when he found these primitive telepaths?'

The realisation that she was still being pursued had given Elizabeth a surge of energy and she had picked up the pace as she hurried down the mountain. But very soon it became clear that the adrenalin rush was short-lived. The cold was soon gripping her tightly and draining her energy. Her feet began to catch on the uneven path as she struggled to lift them.

---

1   See Gary Russell's Tomorrow People novella, *The First One*.

One thing became very clear to her.

She wasn't going to get away from the Yeti on foot.

Elizabeth focused her mind and reached out to John again, hoping to find her friend's thoughts.

There was nothing.

The same, awful dulling effect was there in her mind.

She needed to find another way to send a message. To let John know she was here. She had seen Mike dragged in, wearing thick climbing clothes. The others *must* have known about this area, and they'd be looking at it.

There had to be a way to contact them, to let them know where she was.

But what could she use? There was nothing on the mountains but snow.

Snow.

The Yeti were getting closer. Elizabeth could hear them again.

A wry smile spread across her face. Under normal circumstances she would never have considered doing what she was about to do. She would have thought it feeble and weak, but for now it was the only weapon she had available.

Elizabeth screamed.

Louder and longer than she could have ever imagined possible, she screamed.

The Yeti were drawn to the sound and turned the curve in the path behind her.

Just as their eyes settled on Elizabeth a louder, more ominous sound filled the air. A vast, deep cracking sound.

The ground shook.

An instant later, another crack filled the air and this time the whole mountain began to vibrate.

Looking up the mountain past the Yeti, Elizabeth could just see that her plan had worked. A wall of snow was beginning to cascade down the side.

Her scream had started an avalanche.

4: To Move a Mountain

The blizzard swept in, briefly obscuring the avalanche from view, but Elizabeth could hear the roar of the snow cascading down the mountainside, and she could feel the ground beneath her shaking.

The Yeti also understood what was happening. Panic appeared in their eyes, but Elizabeth wasn't looking at them. She desperately needed to find some kind of shelter. The side of the path had developed a little wall of ice and snow, as the wind had blown fresh falls onto the ridge and compressed it. Extremely fortunately, there was a naturally formed recess in the ice wall just ahead and Elizabeth threw herself into it, hoping it would protect her. She braced herself for the onslaught of the tumbling snow, relieved that she hadn't seen any villages nearby below.

It hit seconds later, filling the air with a choking thick white cloud of snow and ice.

Elizabeth turned her head to the icy wall and closed her eyes, listening to the deafening rumble of the avalanche as it hurtled by her little refuge. She screwed her eyes even more tightly shut and tried not to breathe in the clouds of snow.

The avalanche seemed to last forever, with more and more snow hurtling by.

She wasn't sure it was ever going to stop.

Finally, eventually, the awful noise began to lessen, and the storm of the avalanche grew lighter. Less snow flew past, and the mountain stopped shaking.

Slowly, Elizabeth turned away from the ice and tried to turn around. Her movement was limited by the weight of snow pressing against her, but she wasn't completely enclosed. The snow outside only closed over the little alcove up to her shoulders. Desperately, she began alternately pushing and clawing at the snow to make herself a channel out onto the mountainside. She tried to dig her feet into the snow, to push her way out but it was loose, and she began to slide back in.

Two enormous hands clutched at her shoulders and Elizabeth found herself being heaved easily out of the little niche by one of the Yeti. It looked even wilder than it had before, with thick snow matted into its shaggy fur. It glared at her with baleful eyes, and behind it she saw the second Yeti nursing an apparently broken arm. She felt a brief stab of guilt that her actions had harmed the creature, but she pushed that aside – remembering that these giants were intent on capturing her.

The uninjured Yeti threw Elizabeth across its shoulder and began to trudge its way back up the mountain through the snow.

It was uncomfortable but Elizabeth had to accept that it was easier for her – she probably didn't have the strength or endurance to make it back up to the cave.

She relaxed and just hoped that the avalanche would have been spotted.

TIM's voice demanded the attention of everyone in the Lab. 'John, I believe I have some news that is of interest to us.'

'What is it, TIM?' John asked. He recognised the concern in the computer's voice.

'Sensor data from the area of the Himalayas indicate that there has been an avalanche high on Mount Makalu.'

Stephen recognised the name. 'That's the mountain where the Yeti captured Mike.'

John turned to Marchwood. 'And where you went Yeti-hunting, Professor.'

Marchwood recognised the accusation in John's voice and admitted what he knew about the mountain. 'It's where Baines and the Guardians have their base,' he added. 'Far away from humanity.'

'Any idea what caused the avalanche, TIM?' John asked.

'None at this time,' TIM admitted, 'but no-one was expecting or predicting an avalanche as being imminent.'

John nodded. 'These things can be unpredictable.'

'That is very true.'

'Equally, if someone who didn't have their powers was trying to attract our attention... that would be a very big signal,' John mused.

'Too big to miss,' Stephen agreed. 'So, are we going back to the Himalayas?' he asked eagerly.

'I think we have to,' John confirmed.

Stephen was keen to be under way. 'You'll need some winter gear,' he told John.

He stopped as John held up a hand to hold him back. 'But first, I think we need to drop the professor here back at the museum.'

Marchwood shrank back in horror. 'No. I don't want to go back. I'm safer here.' He took a step away. 'I told you things. About Baines and his people. He'll hurt me for doing that.' He looked genuinely terrified.

John offered a tight, humourless smile. 'Trust me, Professor. We know what we're doing. It's for the best.'

Minutes later, John and Steven materialised in Professor Marchwood's office, holding an unconscious professor between them. They heaved him into the chair behind the desk and settled him as comfortably as they could.

'Here we are,' John said, ensuring that the professor didn't slide in his chair.

Stephen looked around uncomfortably, obviously concerned that they might be caught. 'Are you sure this is a good idea?'

John didn't answer the question directly. Instead, he said sourly, 'It was a waste of time taking him.'

Stephen agreed. 'I know, he was too scared to say anything.'

John gave the professor a withering look. 'He was of no use to us so there's no point in hanging on to him.' He stepped away from Marchwood. 'Right, let's go.'

A familiar voice came from the doorway. 'Not so fast.'

The professor's assistant stood in the doorway, a small box in his hand.

'Baines,' John said nervously.

Baines glared at the two Tomorrow People with a mixture of hatred and disgust. 'It was rude to leave without saying hello.' He flipped the switch on the box he was holding.

Immediately, John and Stephen both released loud groans, their eyes glazed, and they collapsed to the floor.

There was real contempt in Baines's face as he stared at the unconscious telepaths. 'You really shouldn't have come back here. Did you think I wouldn't be waiting?'

'Baines?' Professor Marchwood's voice croaked roughly from his chair.

Baines glanced across at Marchwood with no concern for him at all. 'Professor, you're awake.'

Marchwood pushed himself woozily to his feet. 'They just made me sleep for a few moments.'

'What did you tell them?'

Marchwood shrank under Baines's aggressive stare. 'Nothing. Nothing at all,' he wheedled. 'I wouldn't dare.'

Baines seemed to believe that. He had worked hard to make Marchwood very frightened of him. 'Very wise. Where did they take you?'

'I don't know where it was,' Marchwood answered honestly.

'It doesn't matter,' Baines said dismissively. 'They'll tell us. We'll squeeze it out of them, one way or another.' He sounded like he was going to enjoy making his prisoners talk.

'What are you going to do with them?' Marchwood asked timidly.

'Interrogate them, of course,' Baines barked. A vicious smile curled his lips. *'Thoroughly.'*

Mike had made a complete circuit of his cell, searching for a way to escape, but had no success.

The cell's door was yanked open and two surly guards aggressively shoved a familiar figure into the little room.

'Elizabeth!'

'Mike!' Elizabeth looked relieved to see her friend was unharmed. 'Are you okay?'

'Yeah,' Mike answered as the heavy door was slammed shut. 'Don't like my digs much.'

Elizabeth grimaced. 'I didn't care for the room they gave me either, so I left.'

That make Mike chuckle. 'I thought it was you who'd caused trouble.'

'That's usually *your* department,' Elizabeth said wryly, sitting on the edge of the bed and rubbing her hands together to get some heat back into them.

Mike moved closer and lowered his voice, aware of the shadowy shape of a guard's head present on the far side of the door. 'How did you escape?' he asked.

Elizabeth told him quickly then shook her head sadly. 'I don't think we can use that ploy again,' she said. She bobbed her head towards the door. 'They've left a guard outside.'

'Pity,' sighed Mike.

Elizabeth tried to raise his spirits. 'It's not all bad news,' she said. 'When I was outside, I think I may have brought us some attention.'

Mike had certainly noticed the earlier disturbance. 'All that shaking?'

'I caused an avalanche.' Elizabeth sounded thoroughly pleased with herself.

Mike thought about this. 'If Stephen escaped off the mountain, the avalanche might help them close in on us a bit more.'

'Let's hope so,' Elizabeth sighed. She picked the rough blanket from the bed and wrapped it round her shoulders.

Mike plonked himself down on the other end of the bed. 'So, what are we going to do?'

Elizabeth blew on her hands. 'Once I've defrosted a bit, we're going to start thinking about how we escape from here.'

In the control room of the mountain complex, four figures blinked into existence in the transmaterialisation alcove. Baines and Marchwood stood over the slumped figures of John and Stephen.

Marchwood staggered out of the alcove and leaned heavily on a console. 'Oh, I'm never going to get used to that.'

There was no sympathy forthcoming from Baines. 'Stop complaining, Professor.'

Marchwood wilted under the scorn. 'I'm sorry,' he bleated. 'Do you need my help to move these two?'

Baines dismissed the idea of Marchwood doing something so physical. 'No.'

Marchwood took the insult and shuffled toward the door. 'Oh, alright. I'll get out of the way.'

'Yes.' Baines waved him away and barely saw the professor leave the room. He was more interested in summoning two uniformed guards and pointing them at John and Stephen. 'Take these two to the interrogation room. I want them strapped in before they wake. And then they'll continue to sleep in stasis forever.'

Professor Marchwood left the control room and turned into the rough corridor outside. The guards he passed looked at him with ill-concealed disdain, but they let him go. They knew that he was controlled by Baines. They knew that he was the property of the Guardians.

They knew that he was a traitor to his own kind.

Marchwood walked along the corridor, ignoring the activity around him. He kept his shoulders slumped and his face down, avoiding eye contact as he passed more guards. Then, further on, past one guard standing outside a rough wooden door. He walked by, for five or six paces, before turning sharply. The guard didn't have enough time to see the stun gun in Marchwood's hand before a single shot dropped him where he stood.

Marchwood quickly released the lock and pushed the door open, before peering nervously inside. 'Hello?'

Elizabeth stood up from the edge of the bed, surprised by the identity of the visitor. 'Professor?'

Mike glared at Marchwood accusingly. 'So, *you're* why we're here?'

Marchwood sighed. 'Yes,' he admitted, 'but your friends are why *I'm* here.'

Elizabeth took a step towards Marchwood, concerned something might have happened to John and Stephen. 'What does that mean?'

After looking nervously into the corridor, Marchwood started dragging the stunned guard into the cell. 'It means I could do with some help to get this fellow in here.'

Elizabeth was sceptical of Marchwood's ability to knock out that huge muscular guard. 'How did you do that?'

It dawned on Marchwood that he hadn't explained anything at all well. He pulled a pair of stun guns from inside his jacket and a pair of the newly improved jaunting belts from his pockets. 'John told me to give you these.'

Elizabeth took a belt – in her specific design – and a stun gun. 'We've got belts already,' she said in confusion.

'Apparently, these protect you from the suppression field,' Marchwood explained as best he could. 'Don't ask me how.'

'Do they restore our powers?' Mike asked, putting the new belt on.

'No, but you'll get them back when we completely disable this complex,' the professor told him.

Elizabeth had also pulled on the new belt. 'I tried to do that earlier.'

'That was you, was it?' Marchwood said, appreciatively. 'You caused them a lot of trouble.'

'Not enough,' Elizabeth disagreed.

On his way out of the control room, Marchwood had seen first-hand those earlier efforts by Elizabeth's. 'No, you attacked the power relay system,' he said. 'The real damage has to be done in the generation room.'

Elizabeth's head tilted hopefully. 'And you know where that is?'

'Oh, yes,' Marchwood answered easily. 'I have the run of this place.'

'Very friendly.' Mike didn't try to disguise his disgust for Marchwood.

The professor automatically defended himself. 'Not really,' he answered. 'They despise me, but they know I'm helping them. Or at least I was.'

Elizabeth was not convinced. 'And now you're helping us?'

'Why?' Mike demanded.

'Because it's right.' Marchwood tried to make his actions sound heroic but the faces looking at him were not persuaded. He sighed and admitted, 'And because I can't stand doing this anymore. I just can't take it. John told me we could stop it.'

His desperation seemed to convince Elizabeth and Mike.

'Where is John?' Elizabeth demanded.

Marchwood answered swiftly. 'Oh, he and Stephen are Baines's prisoners... well, sort of.'

Baines sent two guards out of the room about an errand and then sent two more towards John and Stephen, who were still behind him on the floor. 'Take them to the interrogation room. I want to scan their minds.' There was no sound of movement. 'I said take them to the…'

He stopped as he heard the sound of bodies hitting the floor.

'I'm sorry,' John said with studied politeness, 'where did you say you wanted us to go?'

Baines turned and saw John and Stephen standing over his fallen guards. The two Tomorrow People each held a gun of some sort. 'That's impossible,' Baines hissed. 'You were unconscious. I did it myself.'

The lack of foresight shown by Baines really seemed to offend John. 'You don't really think we'd walk into such an obvious trap unprepared, do you?'

Stephen picked up on John's disappointment. 'That's quite insulting, really,' he said.

'Yes, it is,' John agreed.

'We're protected from your little gadget,' Stephen told Baines.

John completed the explanation. 'We just needed you to bring us here.'

Baines refused to be cowed. 'So, what are you going to do?' he asked. 'Kill me?'

John's face contorted into a distasteful sneer. 'No, we don't kill people.'

He squeezed his trigger and the stun gun in his hand flared. Baines dropped heavily to the floor.

'We do stun them though,' he said with a satisfaction that surprised Stephen.

Professor Marchwood had led Elizabeth and Mike through the complex of tunnels to a room which was marked with a form of writing and symbols none of them could read. The stark nature of the lightning flash motif around the room was a clear warning that this was a dangerous part of the energy supply.

Elizabeth was first to decipher the warning symbol. 'So, this is where all the power in the complex comes from?'

'Exactly,' Marchwood confirmed.

Mike looked blankly at the power equipment. 'How do we switch it off?'

Marchwood's lips pursed, and he shrugged. 'I don't know.'

That took Elizabeth by surprise. 'Did you mention that to John?'

'No,' Marchwood shook his head. 'I assumed you would know.'

'Never assume. It makes an…' Mike started an old joke he'd seen on TV.

Elizabeth cut the joke short. The look she gave Mike told him that she knew the punchline and didn't quite approve. 'What about if we just pull everything? Every wire and connection?' she asked.

Mike smirked at Elizabeth's reaction to his joke and accepted her suggestion. 'Seems like a good idea to me.'

'I don't know what will happen, but I can't think of a better idea,' Marchwood admitted.

All three started tearing cables and connections free from the various consoles.

Baines woke up to find his hands tightly bound behind his back. His guards were also securely tied up. John and Stephen were standing watch over him. He was confused and nauseous, but a question forced its way out. 'How did you manage to…'

He trailed off, as the answer was obvious. 'You persuaded Marchwood to help you.'

'It wasn't that difficult,' John confirmed.

'No,' Marchwood said bitterly, 'he's a very easily led man.' He eyed his captors for a moment. 'You know that you still can't use your unnatural abilities.'

'Natural for us,' Stephen said, gripping his stun gun a little tighter.

'Just as fear is unfortunately natural for you,' John told Baines, with something close to pity.

'Of course we fear you,' Baines snapped. 'You have abilities we can never have. We can never compete with you.'

'Why compete?' John asked simply. 'Why not co-operate?'

The idea seemed utterly preposterous to Baines. 'You can't be that naïve.'

John sighed heavily, looking thoroughly disgusted by the reply. 'It's disappointing you're so cynical.' He waved a hand round, indicating the control room and the complex beyond. 'You're going to stand down this little operation of yours and get off Earth.'

Almost in time with John speaking, the lights in the control room died along with the dull background whine of energy. A second later, a low-level emergency light flickered into life.

Baines had tried to scramble to his feet in the confusion, but John's stun gun hadn't moved and was still aimed at him. 'Don't try to run, Mr Baines – or whatever your name really is.'

Baines listened intently, aware that there was now no noise in the complex. 'What have you done?'

'*We* haven't done anything.' Stephen grinned smugly. 'But Professor Marchwood might have.' His smile grew wider as he heard a familiar voice in his head.

'John?'

'Elizabeth!' John and Stephen thought in unison.

'How are you?' John asked telepathically.

Elizabeth's voice returned quickly. 'We're fine.'

'We?' Stephen asked hopefully.

Mike's thoughts sounded in their minds. 'I'm here, too.'

'Good to hear you're okay,' Stephen replied in relief.

Despite sharing Stephen's relief that their friends were safe, John returned his thoughts to business at hand. 'I assume the power cut is your doing?'

'We're British,' Elizabeth answered. 'We're used to power cuts.' They could almost hear her smile.

Mike filled in more detail. 'We've taken down all of their power systems.'

'Baines seems to be taking that badly,' Stephen answered.

John hadn't moved his eyes from their captive. The man's attitude had changed. The smug confidence had gone, replaced by a genuine fear. 'Yes, I might ask him about that,' John thought to the other Tomorrow People, before speaking out loud to Baines. 'Something bothering you, Mr Baines?'

'Our power is off completely,' Baines said. John had been right. The man was undeniably terrified.

'Yes, I know,' John answered.

Despite his hands being bound, Baines tried to squirm up to his feet. 'We have to get out of here.'

'Why?' asked Stephen, suspiciously.

Baines stared at the younger man as if he was an idiot. 'Because if Marchwood has taken all the power off, this mountain will explode in minutes.'

'What?' John barked.

Baines looked desperately from John to Stephen and back again. 'We have a reactor buried deep in the mountain, but we need the power on to keep its core cooled.'

'How bad will it be if it *does* go up?' John demanded.

Baines shook his head. All he could do was give a best guess. 'The top of the mountain will disintegrate,' he said. 'For fifty miles around, maybe a hundred, the snow will cause untold damage. There will be avalanches but, closer to the explosion, the snow will melt and cause floods. Thousands, millions will die.'

'How do we stop it?' John asked urgently. 'How do we save these people?'

Baines scowled in reply. 'What do you care about them?'

'They're innocent people!' John snapped.

'Yes, they are,' Baines answered. 'They're not dangerous like you. We have no quarrel with most people on Earth.'

John met the alien's gaze levelly. 'Only us.'

Baines didn't back down. 'Yes.'

John shook his head as if burying his anger with Baines for the present. 'We'll deal with that after we stop the mountain from detonating.' He waved a hand at Baines's back and the ropes fell from the man's wrists. 'Lead the way.'

Baines rubbed at his wrists, surprised to have been released. 'I shall.'

'And please don't try anything silly,' John added with a hint of menace.

Baines led them into the corridors outside of the control room, past the equipment Elizabeth had sabotaged earlier, and on out into the wider complex of tunnels. 'This way.'

Abruptly the dull lights brightened.

'What's that?' Stephen asked.

'Auxiliary power,' Baines supplied. 'It's taken over from the emergency power, but it'll provide minimum lighting for a short while, nothing else.'

Three figures hurried through the gloom towards them. Stephen and John readied their stun guns but relaxed with relief at the sight of familiar faces.

'Elizabeth!' John beamed.

Elizabeth returned the relieved smile. 'Hello.'

'Are you all right, Mike? I'm so sorry for leaving you.' Stephen burbled, anxiously.

'I'm fine,' Mike answered. 'Glad you made it back to get the cavalry, though.'

John brought the happy reunion back to reality. 'But nobody for hundreds of miles around will fine be in a few minutes,' he said. 'The reactor at the core of the mountain is going to blow up.'

'Because of what we did?' Elizabeth asked, suddenly feeling overwhelmed with guilt.

John dismissed her concern. 'It wasn't your fault. You couldn't have known. It was my plan, not yours. If anyone is to blame, it's me.'

'Then, what are we going to do?' Elizabeth asked.

'Stop it blowing up somehow?' John said hopefully.

Elizabeth caught his arm. 'There's something else.'

John's eyebrows rose. 'Isn't there always?'

'There are children in some sort of suspended animation chambers,' Elizabeth explained. 'With the power off we'll have to help resuscitate them.'

'They're the early telepaths,' Marchwood explained. 'The ones Baines found.'

John grabbed Baines by the arm. 'Can you revive them?'

Baines refused to give an answer. 'I…'

John was not prepared to waste time. 'Look, I don't care what you think of telepaths. Those are *people* you have in stasis.'

'They're children,' Elizabeth added.

It was Professor Marchwood who made the move to persuade Baines. 'I'll make sure he helps,' Marchwood said, aiming a stun gun at Baines.

John gently pushed the stun gun's muzzle towards the ground. 'No violence, professor,' he said firmly. 'That's not how we operate.'

Stephen could see that time was being wasted. 'Mike and I will deal with this,' he said to John. 'You go and sort out that reactor.'

John accepted the suggestion. 'Good luck,' he said to Stephen and Mike.

Marchwood took that as his cue to lead Stephen, Mike and Baines away. 'This way.'

Left alone, John indicated for Elizabeth to lead the way. 'After you, Elizabeth.' They set off down together. Taking note of the heavy woollen sweater she had picked up earlier at the camp, he added 'Love the new look, by the way, The jumper is very you.'

Elizabeth didn't bother looking back. 'Am I really taking fashion advice…'

'…from a fuddy-duddy?' John finished for her, chuckling. 'Point taken.'

Elizabeth took a left turn into another corridor. 'Come on. It's back this way.'

They stopped in their tracks as a ferocious, animalistic roar filled the corridor. Ragged, inhuman breathing came from the shadows ahead.

'What's that?' John asked, in shock more than curiosity. He already knew what he would see. There were giant creatures, somewhere between man and ape, covered with thick white fur, peering at them from the shadows. 'I don't believe it,' he breathed.

Elizabeth obviously recognised the creatures who had captured her. 'Yeti. Be careful,' she warned. 'They're wild.'

'Wouldn't you be, after being locked up for decades?' John answered.

'How do we get past them?' Elizabeth asked. 'I suppose we could stun them.' She didn't sound keen on that idea.

'Or make peace with them,' John suggested. 'I mean, they *are* telepathic.'

Elizabeth was surprised by that revelation. 'They are?'

'I'll explain all that later,' John told her. 'Let's see if we can calm them.'

John and Elizabeth let their minds touch and then reached out to the Yeti.

As a reflex, the minds of the Yeti withdrew and pulled away from this intrusion. A cluttered mess of uncontrolled emotions came from the creatures, threatening to overwhelm John and Elizabeth. They steadied their minds and held their defences in place, pressing gently into the consciousnesses of the Yeti.

Individual personalities began to emerge, memories, warmth, a sense of family and community. Their minds felt almost human.

'They're peaceful,' John said quietly.

Elizabeth nodded. 'And they're frightened.'

John winced as one of the Yeti had an unhappy memory. 'Baines tormented them.'

'Tortured them,' Elizabeth corrected. She had also experienced that memory, and she had felt the pain inflicted on the Yeti. She began to respond telepathically with relaxing thoughts. 'We need to let them know we don't mean them any harm. Let them know we're friends.' In the mix of memories, she found what felt like the laughter of a Yeti and reflected it back at the hairy giants.

'Is it working?' John asked.

'I'm not sure,' Elizabeth answered honestly. 'They're wary of us.'

John had also felt the thawing in attitude from the Yeti, but he had no way of knowing exactly what that meant. 'But will they let us pass?'

Elizabeth thought briefly. 'They know I was a captive like them, so they might. Perhaps if I shared the idea of fear with them, that they need to get away from here…'

She closed her eyes, focusing her thoughts on the need to escape and projected them to the Yeti.

The Yeti began to relax. Warily, John and Elizabeth moved towards them.

Mike and Stephen's little party had reached the room containing the teenagers in stasis caskets. Both Mike and Stephen had to choke down on their disgust at what was being done to these children. They would save their anger for later. The important thing was saving these telepaths.

'These machines,' Mike said to Baines. 'How do they work?'

'They don't,' Baines answered slowly. 'The power is off.'

Stephen didn't fall for the evasion. 'He means, how do they open?'

Marchwood beat Baines to the answer. 'There's a catch on the side.'

Stephen examined the catch and tried to release it but without any success. 'I can't get it to open.'

Marchwood glared at his former assistant. 'Baines. You can do it.'

Baines set his chin resolutely. 'No. I can't.'

'Do it.' Marchwood hefted the stun gun threateningly at Baines.

'It's not that I won't,' Baines said, as if he was talking to a particularly dim child. 'I *can't*. The release requires energy.'

Stephen waved his friend forward. 'Mike, this is your kind of thing.'

'Thanks a lot,' Mike pretended to grumble. '*Get Mike to open the locks.* That's what got me involved with you lot in the first place.' There was truth in what Mike had said. He had been found by criminals while breaking out and forced to take part in bank robberies. Thankfully he had been found by the Tomorrow People before he could get in too much trouble.

Stephen was used to Mike complaining about being the resident lock-pick. 'Oh, stop moaning and open the chamber.'

Mike had already slipped his mind inside the locking mechanism, feeling the different moving pieces and seeing them in his thoughts. 'It's pretty complicated. I can feel it, though.' There was a catch… 'If I… there.'

There was a *click* and *hiss,* and the front of the cabinet swung outwards.

'Well done,' Stephen said enthusiastically.

Marchwood moved to gently took the hands of the teenage girl inside and helped her to step out of the cabinet. Her legs shook like a newborn lamb and she was clearly terrified. 'There, let me help you out,' Marchwood said, in his most encouraging voice. 'Come along.'

The girl tried to speak but her throat sounded

dry, and she barely croaked out her attempt at words.

'What language is that?' Mike asked.

'I'm not sure,' Stephen answered. 'We might need TIM's help with this.'

Stephen tried contacting the girl telepathically. 'Hello. Do you understand me?'

The girl frowned but she looked directly at Stephen.

'She doesn't understand what you said but she knows it's you,' Mike thought.

The girl's eyes snapped towards Mike. She looked from Mike to Stephen with confusion and perhaps a hint of hope, before she spoke again. This time her voice was clearer but neither Stephen nor Mike understood the language she was speaking.

TIM came to their rescue. 'Ah,' he sounded confident in their thoughts. 'I recognise the Chinese dialect. Help the others. I will explain what is happening to our new friend.'

'Thanks, TIM,' Stephen said.

Mike was already holding hand near the lock of the second casket, releasing the mechanism. 'It's much easier once you've done one. It's just knowing where the release mechanism is.'

'Keep going,' Stephen said. 'I don't think we have long.' On cue, the room – and it felt like the whole mountain – shook violently. 'In fact, I'm sure we don't.'

John looked around the power room with dismay. Wires, cable, tubes and connections of every sort had been pulled out of all the machines. 'Well, you did plenty of damage in here, didn't you?' he said to Elizabeth.

She simply shrugged. 'Your plan, remember.'

'I know,' John murmured, weighing up the destruction. 'There's nothing we can do here. Just re-attaching systems won't be enough – not in the time we have left anyway.'

Elizabeth had expected the machinery in the room to be beyond repair and was already searching for alternatives. She had found a doorway which led deeper into the complex and which had the same warning symbols as the room they were in.

She rapped on the door to attract John's attention. 'Looks like the power generator is this way.'

'Let's have a look at it.'

They hurried into the corridor.

Mike was working fast at freeing the young telepaths from their cabinets. They were all awake and those still inside the cabinets looked close to panic. Marchwood was helping to calm the others.

Raising his hand Mike began to release the lock on another casket. 'Just two more to go.'

Stephen reached out to the Lab. 'Are you communicating with them, TIM?'

TIM replied immediately. 'They are frightened, but they seem to understand that you are there to help.'

'That's something,' Stephen said.

Mike stepped away from the casket and swung the door open. The inhabitant was the groovy girl who was apparently from the 1960s, according to her attire. He looked round to find someone to help her step out, and noticed someone was missing. 'Where's Baines?'

Marchwood looked around. He looked guilty and annoyed with himself. 'He must have slipped out when I was looking after these young people.'

Stephen frowned. 'Where would he go?'

The corridor Elizabeth had found led to the chamber holding the generators. They were huge coils of metal, reaching from floor to ceiling, and had countless other small pieces of machinery and control panels all around them. A large purple door marked with the danger symbol was at the far end of the room.

'Do you understand this technology?' Elizabeth asked, more in hope than anything else.

John gave an honest – and depressing – answer. 'Not even slightly.' He looked to a dial which was heading into an area marked in purple. 'I do know that looks like an overload.'

'It is,' Baines's voice came from behind them. 'Let me see.' He pushed his way through to the panel John had indicated.

'Well?' John demanded.

Baines shook his head. His face was ashen. 'There's no way to avoid an explosion without realigning all of the circuits through one rotation, in order.' He pointed at the purple door. 'In there.'

John was already making for the door. 'Let's get on with it.'

Baines caught his arm. 'If you go inside the energy will reduce you to atoms.'

Elizabeth didn't see a problem. 'We'll do it from out here.'

Baines glanced quickly at one of the read-outs and shook his head. 'There won't be time.'

John only hesitated a moment. 'Get your people as far from here as you can,' he said. 'We'll try to sort this.'

Baines looked at him in shock. 'You'll be killed.'

'Probably,' John agreed, 'but there's a chance we can do it.' He reached out telepathically to Mike. 'Have you got those children free?'

Mike's voice sounded in his head an instant later. 'Yes.'

'Get them back to the Lab,' John instructed.

'Will do,' Mike agreed.

Stephen cut in, sounding concerned, 'What about you?'

'We'll see you in the Lab,' John answered.

'I hope,' Elizabeth added, before she and John turned their attention to the purple door.

Stephen had contacted TIM as soon as Elizabeth had finished speaking. 'We're going to need some extra belts for these kids.'

'Sending them now,' TIM replied smoothly.

Sure enough, a few seconds later, a pile of belts shimmered into existence on the floor in front of the released children. They were an equal mixture of fascinated and terrified.

Mike and Stephen quickly began handing out the belts and indicating how they should be worn. They weren't regular jaunting belts and TIM would control the jaunt, but they *were* exactly what was needed.

While John tried to see and feel inside the equipment beyond that purple door, Elizabeth was surprised to see Baines was still there with them. 'What are you still doing here? Get your people out. You have matter transporters.'

'They won't have any power,' John murmured, only half listening to her.

On this occasion, though, John was wrong. 'They have an emergency battery circuit,' Baines said. 'Just enough power to get us out.'

'Then go,' Elizabeth urged.

Baines took a step towards the door and then stopped. 'Come with us,' he said, reaching a hand back to Elizabeth and John.

'We don't need to,' Elizabeth reminded him.

Baines looked like he was going to say something, as if he wanted or needed to say something, but instead he turned and ran.

John's focus was now entirely on the machinery that was out of sight beyond the ominous purple door. 'Right,' he told Elizabeth. 'We need to do this quickly, but we can't start a circuit till the previous one has stopped moving.'

Elizabeth could see and feel the machinery as John shared his thoughts with her. 'I'm ready.'

The Lab was full.

It had never been intended for so many people but, as well as Mike and Stephen, it now held Professor Marchwood and the seven released telepaths, all of whom were coping with at least some level of trauma.

'We need an extension on the Lab,' Stephen muttered.

Professor Marchwood was aware that not everyone had made it back to the Lab. 'Where are John and Elizabeth?'

'They're trying to stop the mountain exploding,' Mike answered.

'Hundreds of thousands will die if they fail,' TIM added gloomily.

Stephen gnawed nervously on his bottom lip. 'They can't have long left.'

TIM's voice rang inside John's head. 'John, can you hear me?'

John barely paid the computer any heed. 'Bit busy just now, TIM.'

'You must remember your own safety,' TIM warned. Concern for his friends was clear in his voice.

Elizabeth and John worked in unison to operate another level of realigning the circuits. 'There's still a chance to put this right.'

TIM was compelled to give a stark warning. 'If you can't, you will have only a fraction of a second to jaunt out.'

John's reply sounded far more irritated than he intended. 'We'd be a lot quicker if you weren't distracting us.'

TIM didn't take any offence. 'Is there any way I can help?'

'Sorry, TIM,' John answered. 'This is down to us.'

The atmosphere in the Lab had grown unbearably tense. Even the young, unfrozen telepaths were on edge, though they didn't know exactly why. They just knew that their rescuers were desperately worried about something.

'How long have they got left?' Professor Marchwood asked. His voice was tight and choked.

'Under fifteen seconds,' TIM replied instantly.

'They need to get out of there,' Mike whispered.

'They won't leave while there's a chance,' Stephen said.

'Eight seconds,' TIM updated them.

Mike's fingers had started tapping nervously on the table. 'TIM, can you jaunt them out?'

Stephen cut that idea down. 'It's not what they want…'

TIM agreed with him. 'John was clear that I should leave them.'

'How long?' Marchwood's voice was barely a whisper.

'Three seconds,' TIM replied, 'two, one…'

Mike winced as the countdown reached zero.

No-one spoke until a voice came from the jaunting pad.

'What's with the screwed-up faces?' Elizabeth asked.

She and John made their way from the pad to the table.

'If the wind changes, your face will stay like that,' John told Mike.

The younger man just laughed in relief. 'You did it!'

'Yes, we did,' John said and then took a deep, relieved breath. 'With half a second to spare. We'll try to cut it even finer next time.'

Elizabeth took a seat. 'I could really use a cup of tea please, TIM.'

'I think we should talk to Mr Baines first,' John said. He was clearly not finished with that part of the problem.

'Is he still on the mountain?' Stephen asked.

'No, he got his people away,' Elizabeth answered.

'But I'm sure TIM knows where they are,' John said glancing up at the pleasantly pulsing lights above.

'Indeed I do,' TIM answered.

Baines and his people had not teleported as they had expected to their spaceship, a boring and grey construction which was entirely functional and lacking in any kind of pleasing aesthetic design. Instead, at John's request TIM had diverted their matter transporter to the thankfully closed Natural History Museum, as a sort of neutral ground, where they could meet the Tomorrow People.

'You managed to repair the reactor,' Baines said. It was unsure if it was a statement or a question.

John gave a slight grimace in reply. 'I wouldn't go that far.'

'We managed to stop it blowing up,' Elizabeth expanded. 'That's enough for us.'

John took over again. 'It will be dismantled, and the caves returned to their natural state – or as close as possible.'

'And what will happen to us?' Baines asked.

'What do you mean?' John frowned.

Baines looked around the museum. 'This isn't a jail but we are your prisoners.' His eyebrows rose questioningly. 'Will you execute us? Put us into stasis?'

John was appalled by the suggestions. 'Oh, good grief, no.'

'That's not our way,' Elizabeth said rather more warmly.

Baines was still uncertain. 'Then what?'

John sighed. 'You're going home.'

Elizabeth explained a bit more fully. 'The telepaths you put in stasis need long-term help to recover from the ordeal. They must come to terms with a lot. Not just their abilities but also with the fact that the world they knew is gone, and everyone they knew is either old or dead.'

'And all because they had *mild* telepathic powers,' John made no attempt to hide his anger at that. 'None of them were even fully Tomorrow People.'

Elizabeth took over again, aware that her calm attitude was less likely to cause friction than John's annoyance. 'The Galactic Federation will have representatives here in a few minutes. They're going to collect them and give them the therapy they need. They'll be doing the same for the Yeti,' she added, rather amused by the idea of the Yeti wandering around a Federation space station.

John nodded. 'While they're here, they'll be picking your people up and taking you back home as part of the opening of diplomatic negotiations with your planet.'

Baines simply shook his head. 'My people won't listen.'

'They might,' John said firmly, 'if you support the Federation.'

Baines looked at John as if he was mad. 'I can't.'

Elizabeth maintained that calm, level voice she had learned at teaching college. She had always thought it was for boisterous pupils, not for galactic diplomacy. 'You were surprised we didn't kill you. Why?'

'Because we did all of this to you,' Baines answered simply. 'And we put hundreds of thousands at risk.'

'But you didn't kill the telepaths when you caught them,' John cut in quickly. 'Why was that?'

The answer seemed obvious to Baines. 'Because it's not a civilised thing to do.'

'Exactly,' John answered simply. 'That's why we don't kill.'

Baines wasn't convinced. 'Even if other humans do?'

'We strive to make humanity better, more advanced,' Elizabeth explained, 'and that's not just about our powers.'

'It's up to you whether you help us or not,' John said. 'We're sending you home safe either way.'

John and Baines looked at each other hard, each man weighing up the other and trying to work out what the outcome of this meeting would mean, or more importantly, what it *could* mean.

'I'll help,' Baines said abruptly. He said it quickly, as if he worried he might change his mind if he waited any longer. 'It won't be easy, but I'll help.'

'Thank you,' John sighed. 'That's a bit of a relief.' He offered a tight smile. 'If you come back to Earth, come as a friend.'

'I will,' Baines promised.

As Baines moved away to talk to his guards and explain what was to happen next, Stephen and Mike brought Professor Marchwood across to join John and Elizabeth.

'And what about you, Professor?' John asked. 'What's next for you?'

The professor looked around sadly. 'This exhibition will have to come to an end, I suppose.'

'I suppose so,' Elizabeth agreed.

Stephen tried to offer the professor some hope for optimism. 'That doesn't mean your research has to.'

Marchwood thought for a moment. 'No, it doesn't, does it?'

'That's better,' Elizabeth said, enthusiastically.

Marchwood was already running potential plans through his head. 'Did you know that sightings of Bigfoot in America stretch across several states?' He warmed to his subject. 'There have been more sightings in Colorado than in California. Perhaps an expedition there?' He looked at Mike and Stephen. 'You could be of great help to me...'

Mike looked very enthusiastic about the idea. 'I've always wanted to see America.'

'So have I,' Stephen agreed.

John held his hand up to pause the conversation. 'And I think that's our cue to leave.'

Off to the side, representatives of the Galactic Federation began to appear inside the museum.

'I think so too,' Elizabeth agreed.

'Oh.' Marchwood sounded disappointed.

'Good luck, Professor,' John said.

Elizabeth smiled. 'And thank you.'

'Goodbye...' Professor Marchwood began, but the four Tomorrow People had already begun to disappear with Mike's 'bye' only half-said.

Professor Marchwood didn't care. He had seen the most extraordinary things and had rediscovered his urge to explore for the impossible. 'Marvellous.'

The Tomorrow People landed back on the jaunting pad in the Lab.

The young telepaths had already been collected by the Federation. Sooner or later, somebody from the Federation would want a long debrief about what had happened but for now – for once – the Tomorrow People were going to enjoy some well-earned relaxation.

Until the next time they were needed…

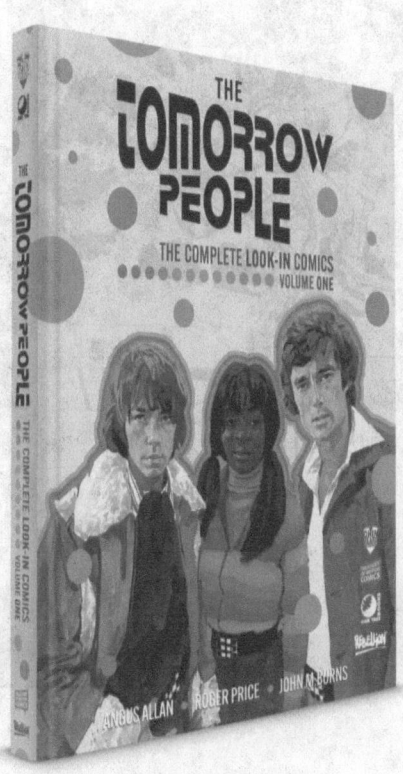

You may also enjoy…